Jenny

CORLD

BY JULIE RUPERT

DORRANCE PUBLISHING CO., INC.
PITTSBURGH, PENNSYLVANIA 15222

Dorrance Publishing Co., Inc.
701 Smithfield Street
Pittsburgh, PA 15222
Visit our website at www.dorrancebookstore.com

ISBN: 978-1-4349-1522-1
eISBN: 978-1-4349-1440-8

Tony and Cassie

"Haven't you finished it yet?" Tony's plaintive accusation rose from the floor where he was slouched, leaning against the bed.

Cassie didn't take her eyes off the computer screen as she calculated and completed the mathematical equation that was Tony's homework. She couldn't help smiling at her success. Tony's maths had looked complicated when he first showed her what he needed to finish, but she once again found one step followed another and as long as the calculations were correct, the equations would work out. This was stuff she wouldn't be doing for another two years. So pleased was she, she forgot to be angry with Tony for his ungrateful impatience.

"This is fun Tony. Even you could do it if you tried."

Tony sank further onto the floor. "No way. It is boring and of no use."

Cassie swiveled the chair round to face him. "But you need to work out sums when you make fireworks. Speed and direction and...um...whatever else you need for your ideas."

Tony got up ready to join her at the desk. "So you have finished. Let's go to that fireworks site now."

Cassie swiftly turned back to the computer. "No. There is still more and I have to do my own homework."

"Aw Cassie. That will be enough. Nobody will expect me to do more anyway." He moved the other chair slightly in front of hers and collapsed into it. Moving her chair to accommodate his, she relinquished control of the screen. She couldn't be bothered to fight him anymore.

Cassie thought of how little of her own homework she had completed, but as she watched Tony's fingers move rapidly and knowingly over the keyboard, she resigned herself to having to get up early in the morning to do it before leaving for school. While she was thinking this, the fireworks site appeared.

"That was quick," she remarked. Tony didn't reply. After all, he had called up the site, so of course it would appear.

Cassie looked at the screen. The background black looked glutinous and seemed to be in motion. From within this mass, colours exploded outwards, some more spectacularly than others. The black mass appeared to fold over any colour that failed to burn brightly across the screen. The site had never introduced itself like this before. She concentrated on the text. Maybe Tony had called up a different site. Her interest in the creation of fireworks was not as intense as his and he may have progressed to more complicated pyrotechnic knowledge since the last time she had watched him. The text however seemed to be distorted in some way. Sentences would not finish, or if they did, they would be in a different context from the beginning. It was also scattered around the screen in a pattern Cassie couldn't follow.

"Look at this." Tony's finger touched the screen, in his excitement forgetting one of rules their parents laid down about looking after the computer. "Somebody has set one firework against another." Tony's eyes followed the text. "But it missed so they are not sure if the firework actually was aiming for the other." He turned to Cassie though talking more to himself. "I hadn't thought of changing the direction that way, by throwing another firework in its path that will attract it."

Cassie was still trying to follow the text that had been under Tony's finger but gave up now it had been explained to her.

"Sounds a bit more complicated than your experiments with aerodynamics and propulsion."

"Maybe," said Tony as he turned back to the screen, "and it would be more fun."

Cassie didn't think it sounded like fun; she thought it was more like aerial warfare. She was losing interest in this, to her eyes, an incoherent site. Then more text appeared, in larger and stable type this time, teasing her to read and understand. She rolled her chair closer, but Tony, to her annoyance was making himself bigger, spreading out so he could command the whole screen. She stubbornly stayed close to him. During the homework session he couldn't get far enough away from the screen. The text had moved away from the edges. She leaned in to follow its course. Flashes of colour seemed to be pushing the words. The reds were magnificent; Cassie had never seen so many brilliant variations. Sometimes the words seemed to be pushed too hard and they sank into the black background but she kept watching and they emerged on other parts of the screen, distorted and trying to regain their shape. The behaviour of the site was compelling. You had to catch the information it contained while a frenetic display of pyrotechnics was also in progress. The text she had been chasing was now blurred behind a diffused glow and reading was made even more difficult by the blinding glare of tiny explosions falling on the words. The letters fell away but Cassie found she could understand them because they were being spoken as well.

"Wow! That was nearly six seconds. I wonder what the mixture was in that one. The flash has to be more though...the aluminum...."

The words petered out to be replaced by chemicals that burned the colours they produce when exposed to heat. Cassie held her finger close to one of the flaming chemicals. It was hot. She looked at Tony. He was peering intently at the screen, his eyes following the action and his lips repeating the information that appeared in the tumult.

"This is a weird site, Tony. Why would something like that be written?" She pointed to the text but it had disappeared. Instead, there was a deep, molten blue blemish rupturing through the black glutinous mass. Cassie was transfixed. If it grew any more, it looked like it would dissolve through the screen. She was startled by a low rumble that she felt go through her and the blue was now being engulfed by the black back-ground. She checked the volume. It wasn't on and Tony had not been using the mouse either. How was the screen moving?

"Are you understanding any of this?" Cassie asked. "I think we should go back to maths or at least the fireworks site you usually visit. At least they make sense."

"No, look. Here is a bit on the mechanics of propulsion, mathematically laid out." Tony, smiling, quickly glanced at Cassie before turning his rapt attention back to the screen.

She leaned forward to follow the line of equations. They looked remarkably like the calculations in Tony's homework. Well, that is a coincidence, Cassie thought. But then, the figures changed and not only were they incomprehensible but the let-ters and numbers were becoming distorted and sliding out of focus. The site was bewildering but she waited, with rapt atten-tion, for the next manifestation. It was another fireworks display with the different types of effects, the Roman candle, the fish, the salute, and it grew, as Tony and Cassie stared, into a billow-ing mass of brilliant white and suddenly erupting from within it, an explosion of stars and sparks, all black. Muffled thunder reverberated round the room.

"How can it be...?" Tony leaned forward for a closer inspection.

"Tony," exclaimed Cassie, "you are blocking...." She stopped as she realized he wasn't blocking her view because she couldn't see him. She could feel his back leaning forward beside her and she put out her hand and took hold of his shirt.

"Tony, what are you doing?" Cassie was shouting in fright. She tightened her grip on his shirt trying to see him, to keep him with her. But it wasn't enough.

There was nothing in the room now except for the home-work bits and pieces lying beside the keyboard in front of the computer. The room was empty and still. The computer screen faded then it lit up the room momentarily as the site for the mathematics homework returned.

Bella

Bella could hear the television now that she had finished clattering around in the kitchen. A news program was on; she could hear the serious tones of the broadcaster. The topic must be of extreme interest if the kids haven't as yet taken the controls from Justin. She hung up the tea towel and went into the living room. Surprisingly, only Justin was sitting in there, comfortable in the quiet of the room, his feet warmed by Queenie, asleep and snoring gently. She kissed Justin on top of his head to lessen the interruption to his viewing.

"The children not down yet?" she queried, though she knew she was stating the obvious.

Justin kept his attention on the TV screen. "No."

Bella curled up on the couch beside him. "They have usually completed their homework by now."

Cassie, she knew, would have finished before dinner, but Tony, using his authority as the older brother, would have cajoled her into helping with his, or even allowed her to do it for him. Bella stood up again.

"I will just check on them."

Justin looked up at her. "They are fine. Any interruption Tony will see as a chance to leave the work completely."

Bella nodded. "Yes, I know." She kept walking towards the stairs. "I will only peep in."

"That is still enough to have him down here wrestling for the control," Justin shouted after her.

She smiled as she went up the stairs. Justin's evening viewing had been saturated lately with episodes of Tony's favourite shows. Presently it is a science fiction saga. To escape, Justin will take Queenie out for walks, only to discover, on return, the episodes are inexhaustible.

Bella approached the closed door of Tony's room. It was very quiet in there. He must be letting Cassie do his work without interrupting with his own interpretations of the subject knowledge. She knocked. There was no answer. She opened the door enough to peep in. The room was empty. Bella looked around as she entered. Everything was still and the silence surrounded her. She tried to listen for their presence outside the room, but there were no thumps of footsteps, no slamming of doors, flushing of the toilet, no shouts of sibling abuse. A flash of light lit at the corner of her eye; the computer screen was still on. She walked to the empty chairs facing the screen. Homework books, mainly mathematics, lay open on one side of the keyboard and on the other side, a notebook with pencils and eraser rested on the open pages. Equations had been calculated, some of the answers worthy of being underlined. Cassie had been busy.

Maybe they had gone out to visit friends, though they didn't tell her of such a plan and she hadn't heard them leave. She listened for their comings and goings all the time, but it could be she missed their going. They were growing up; they did not need constant monitoring—Tony sixteen years and Cassie fourteen years now. Bella knew she worried about them as much as ever, still listening to and observing their activities, surreptitiously always trying to know where they were and what they were doing. She walked out of the room to the top of the stairs, keeping down an inclination to panic.

"Are the kids down there?" she shouted as she started downwards. Reaching the lounge, she could see Justin and Queenie still in the same position, and no one else.

She tried to sound unconcerned. "Do you know where they are, Justin?"

Justin looked back at her and frowned slightly as he noticed her anxiety. "No, but they are okay. Probably just gone outside." He turned his attention back to the television.

Bella climbed the stairs again. She looked in Cassie's room, the bathroom, the study and in her bedroom. She leaned out the window, calling their names. The silence continued and became oppressive as she walked back into Tony's room.

The computer screen flicked light across the room though the screen page didn't change. She sat in one of the chairs, leaning forward to read the text. It was A level mathematics. A few lines of theoretical explanation crossed the screen and underneath were numerals and symbols creating equations. Some of the details looked familiar but Bella knew the whole was not the same mathematics she had studied at school. She had never wondered why this was so, just accepted Tony and Cassie would always know more than her. There was also a fingerprint on the screen. Tony's no doubt, so maybe he did help Cassie after all. She looked past the fingerprint at the symbols. They seemed to be changing. She marveled at the clever imagery, wondering if it did make mathematics easier or at least, more fun to study. She concentrated on the numbers, trying to understand why they changed. A shadow appeared behind the numbers and it was falling. Bella gasped with astonishment as another faint outline appeared, a small hand, trying to grasp something just out of reach. She looked closer, but the numbers were clear now and remained steady. There were no shadows or faint outlines. Bella put her finger up to the screen to trace the pathway of what she thought she had seen. Her finger went through the screen. She snatched her hand away, horrified. The screen had been like hot mud, but now it was unmarked with A level mathematics waiting to be studied.

Bella sat back in the chair and anxiously looked round the room. Tony's unmade bed, clothes on the floor and the open books on aerodynamics and fireworks—what he was truly interested in—took her fright away. Everything was waiting for their return. But where were they? She turned back to the computer. Slowly, she let her fingers touch the screen. They sank in, though it was as if the screen were hardening. It was not so hot, more like cooling, crusty mud now. She pressed harder, her hand disappearing into the screen. It felt like nothing, there was no sense of her hand. Bella stood up, forcing some of her arm further in and now, she felt a slight suction. Before she could properly understand this, the pull became stronger. Becoming frightened, she instinctively dragged her arm out. Suddenly, she was sitting on the floor.

She stared at her hand while trying to steady her breathing. She wondered what that was all about. She was obviously getting herself in a high emotional state over the children and as a consequence, having a turn of some sort. She crouched slowly, ready to stand up, when she noticed the floor. It was not like anything she had seen before. A slight luminosity gave it a blurred finish and it didn't feel very substantial either. She worried if it could support her weight. She was kneeling on it without any trouble even though it felt soft and deep somehow. There wasn't firm support under her knees or hands. She sat back on her heels, wondering how to stop from falling, though that was silly because she wasn't. A light came on suddenly and it was all around her. Her eyes hurt. The light was so bright and the brightness prevented her from seeing past it. She could be in a tiny room or in a large glowing outside.

Squinting relieved the glare and with the violence of the light lessened, she started to hear noises. Vague shadows gave shape to an edge of the light and the sound seemed to be coming from there. She stood but fell down immediately as there was no sensation of a floor. She waited and was relieved when she didn't fall any further. Ignoring the fact she could feel nothing under her feet, Bella tried standing again. That accomplished, she squinted and headed for the shadowed shapes. But it was difficult. There was no solid base on which to put her feet. It was like being very drunk except, as she gratefully found out, hitting the ground was not so painful. She decided to trust the floor to perform its task of being there and told her feet not to be fooled by the absence of support. Her gait was a mixture of stumbles and spasms but she was moving forward.

Suddenly, the light was extinguished though a dimness remained. The change of light disorientated her again and she fell forward, resting on her hands and knees. She raised her head. The shapes were in front of her now, much closer, and she could hear chittering noises, like many unmelodious small birds. Something that looked like a number three approached her awkwardly and a blunt, gentle clamp was placed on her arm. It was tugging her forward. Alarmed at her disorientation and apparent hallucinations, she abruptly stood, swaying with a feeling of nausea. The clamp released her arm and she heard a soft thump. The chittering was more excited now. Looking down, a flat shape—not quite a three—lay at her feet. She watched in astonishment as it rose up to the height of just above her knee and glided away towards the other shapes. She followed it, finding herself amongst equally sized numerals, symbols and equations. It was like an animated textbook. The noises had stopped and she stared at the silent mass below her. It was colourful with a smattering of blue and red through the black and the symbols gave it an interesting form. When she realized she didn't have to squint anymore, italics and more substantial characters emerged. She was looking at all the types found in texts, especially mathematical ones. But there was no understandable order to them. They were just clustered around her.

Bella was finding it difficult to grasp a complete thought. Her mind whirled around trying to find reason or anything that was familiar but what her eyes fed her brain left her numb with incomprehension. She was forced to concentrate though when she heard a recognizable word.

"Who...." Immediately a cacophony of noise started. It was coming from all around her and it was incomprehensible babble. It battered at Bella's veneer of confidence. Suddenly, the voices retreated as something clearly said, "are you."

She waited for more but the protracted query was for her identity. She could feel the expectation of an answer. She wondered how this was working: no mouths to talk or ears to listen and numerals were not supposed to communicate anyway. She stared, but this whole situation was not going away. There was nothing else except the mass of types crowding around her. The question must have come from there. She had best get on with it.

"Bella. My name is Bella."

The pressure of a clamp returned to her lower leg. She saw the numeral 3 had attached its top semi circle to below her knee. She couldn't help a shudder and the strangeness of it had her instinctively flinging her leg to free itself of the clamp. But the 3 had already released its grip.

"Light…," the voice came from 3, but again, it was immediately followed by many others. The word "light" was being echoed in different contexts, light speed, light scribe, light force, when suddenly, the words stopped at the same time as 3 said,

"Stay away from."

The numbers and symbols were quiet now, surrounding her, obviously waiting for her to respond. The number 3 was closest. Its upper curve was arched upwards, towards her. Slowly, she lowered herself and when she could go no further downwards, she sat comfortably with her legs crossed. Number 3 retracted his upper half as she settled herself at his level. He didn't move away, he was just waiting in front of her. She could feel their attention on her. Or she hoped she did, otherwise she was losing her mind. She thought she must be in the computer. How, why…all those questions were irrelevant. She had no idea, she only knew this looked like a computer site and therefore she had to be in one. She shivered with cold. The light was affecting her. It remained dim but it spread steadily around her. There were neither shadows nor an end to it, the light was forever. She heard another word. They may be mathematical types and this all may be her fevered insanity, but she was pleased communication was being attempted. It comforted her. The word had been *why,* and the chittering that followed the utterance had drowned comprehension. Silence fell again and she heard, *are you here.* Of course, this was how the computer spoke. She felt she had an explanation. Computers always tried to conjecture what request would be typed, changing its guess as more letters are added. Bella smiled. Vocalized by many would make any tentative idea disappear into incoherence. She wouldn't be so impatient with the computer's presumptions in future. She remembered the question and her heart stung her.

"My children. I think they are here."

The chittering started again which Bella found interesting as no preceding word had prompted it. She wondered about the possible extent of thought processes and independent conversation of the characters. 3 touched her leg.

"Bring them," he said.

At least they believed her, but could it be so easy to bring them back, she wondered.

"How…." The chittering started immediately. "…to bring them," Bella finished quickly.

"Compulse," 3 replied with the confidence of stating the obvious.

Bella took a deep breath. "What is compulse?"

3 turned away from her to face the now definitely agitated mass. She couldn't know what was happening as she didn't recognize any of the sounds that were blending to create a rising noise. From the mass, a plus sign came out to stand beside 3.

"It is more," he said. The mass seemed satisfied with that and was quiet, waiting for Bella to understand. She didn't and she felt confused and upset. She didn't know where her children were and she couldn't understand anything that was happening. How could she possibly help them? She began to feel afraid but then wondered why. If they were here, Tony especially would think it was a great adventure. This is a computer world and he knows his way around a computer. She has not been so confident but has taught herself how to use one. Not to any great expertise, she admits, but she has been experimenting more as her knowledge of the capabilities of a computer has increased. She will apply the same logic here by searching for the right bit of information. She relaxed as there was no impatience at her slow comprehension and replies. "More of what?" she finally asked.

3 and + talked to each other with contributions from the mass in general. Finally there was a long silence and 3 swelled and contracted as if he was readying himself for a difficult task.

"To go somewhere, we compulse. We begin to feel strong and then we move. Now you compulse to children or compulse children here."

Bella thought about this. It sounds like willing something to happen, which she supposed was how the cursor operated on a computer. Feeling a bit silly, Bella said she would try to compulse her children.

She sat quietly and thought of Tony and Cassie. Were they even here or was this her own personal hallucination? What was happening to her? Whatever it was, some of the fear she held for her mind would be alleviated if the children were with her. That would prove she still had some sanity. Cassie would sit and roll her eyes at Tony's wild ideas on why this situation was great, but Bella remembered it was Cassie who had many times returned home with interesting stories to tell of people she had met while wandering somewhere different. Bella opened her eyes. The children were not here. 3 and + were beside her, blurred through her tears. The mass was still.

"I can't compulse," she explained. Blinking her tears away she continued, "What we do is yell if we need the children to come." She lifted her head and exploded with the noise of their names, except that only a muffled gasp came out. Bella tried again, frustration giving strength to the volume. The mass of types shrank back at her physical display. She felt useless. She couldn't even vent her despair. Looking down at 3 and +, she could finally believe she was in a computer. Yelling at the computer at home didn't make it work faster or more appropriately either.

"Better, maybe, if I was closer to them," Bella offered as an excuse for her failure.

"Where are they?" asked 3.

She leaned closer, dismayed at what she was going to say. "I don't know where they are," she whispered.

Every type heard and it caused general movement but the chittering was subdued.

"What is wrong?" asked Bella.

3 touched her knee. "We not understand... 'not knowing'. We always know where we are."

Bella pondered this. "Are you always here?"

3 spoke again. Bella was becoming used to the way the types communicated. Their conversations were questions and answers with genuine concern for the meanings. There were still hesitation and mutterings while they considered other interpretations but these became less as they grasped the content of the conversation.

"We are compulsed or we are here."

"Can you describe here?" asked Bella.

"Describe?" 3 was silent for a while. "Here is here."

Bella thought they probably only had an awareness of their own presence, not their surrounding environment. But they were aware of each other and they knew she was suddenly in their midst. They also knew she was different and they themselves thought differently otherwise + would not have come out to speak. If they were the same, 3 would speak for them all. For that matter, he couldn't and wouldn't as they would then all speak as one, as a single entity.

While Bella had been thinking this, the types had also been chittering. Now 3 spoke out.

"When not here we are elsewhere. Compulse to where needed." A general clamour of agreement greeted this comment. He continued, "Sometimes, where we are needed, we are not correct." 3 stopped and there was no noise but a shiver went through the mass. "We come back or not."

"How do you mean, 'not correct'?" asked Bella.

+ stretched up, elongating his type. "It is a place where they make us be what we are not."

There was movement at the front of the mass and characters for equations emerged. Bella saw the equal sign, the less than and more than signs and dots that floated around which eventually combined to make a *therefore*. It was *therefore* that spoke, bringing the upper dot closer to Bella.

"The numbers are used to make meanings different but it is impossible for those meanings to be correct. 3 cannot change his value."

3 swivelled his upper circle back to Bella. "We know our value is being altered therefore (at which *therefore* buzzed about importantly, if erratically), we now perceive who we are." 3 paused, thinking of how to express exactly what it was that happened to them. "This other place is not right. It is creating something false and has enabled us to be aware of this." 3 reached out towards Bella though he didn't touch her. He spoke quietly. "You are here where we mean what we are and the children are in that other place."

Bella listened and watched. The mass had, unusually, fallen quiet while 3 was speaking. Some shrank down, giving the mass of form an eroded look. Even + looked diminutive. They were comprehending these other places and sites. Their world has not only expanded suddenly but it has threatened their integrity and existence. They had been used for situations that were wrong, or maybe just used to give a situation viability. They couldn't make sense of it therefore felt useless because they were unable to have meaning. Bella wondered if that meant the situation was wrong. New ideas or new ways of looking at old ideas seem strange at first. But what of sites she knew were wrong and would never visit: the ones that immersed themselves in cruelty to children and animals, the sites that were politically or religiously aggressive, the porn sites; or even the sites that were not obviously malicious but enticed you there and then insidiously set about to keep you returning when there were more important things to do? It was probably easier than people realized. After all, she had wasted more hours than she should, mindlessly playing games. Maybe that was what 3 meant by "compulse". It kept you tapping away and you enter further into the site until it gradually becomes more and more of the world you inhabit. You have to become like that world to be able to inhabit it. Your sense of self disappears, as in an addiction. And cruelty and porn are addictive. The types had become tense as they talked and considered their bigger world. What if this compulse to go to these sites became too strong for them? She shivered. Maybe that was what the types felt—they could become trapped in that place and be changed to mean something not right.

She became aware of the noise they were making. It was definitely a discussion, though becoming heated Bella realized with astonishment. There were interjections, shrill tones now and then, and brief pointed silences. Shuffling amongst them kept the mass in a continual state of movement. She concentrated on listening for words and tones she could understand. The number 8 was out in front of the mass, eagerly talking to 3 and +. Other numbers interrupted and *therefore* was moving his three dots around separately. One dot was just behind 8 and quivering. Another was now slowly moving over 3 and +. 3 swatted at it and it moved swiftly back to the other one. Bella couldn't see the third dot. It looked as if 3 was trying to control the discussion, while + stood quietly but firmly at his side. Bella thought he was in bold. Finally 3 swung around to Bella.

"We have decided," he declared. This complete statement brought forth sudden loud chittering from the mass which confused Bella. 3 waved his upper type at them. "Some are disappointed."

"Disappointed at what?" asked Bella.

"We compulse with you to find the children."

"What, all of you?" exclaimed Bella.

"No. Not all, that is why disappointment. 8 says he has been in nuclear equations and he is a stable number, 5 says you will need strength and he is highest category for hurricanes and no equation will work without the other number parts, so all types are necessary. But we are too many." 3 looked at Bella. "I say all stay here and keep watch. Only + and me, 3, we compulse with you. Is okay?"

Bella was overwhelmed. "It is very kind of you and I am very grateful for the help. Thank you."

+ became even darker and more obvious. "Cannot have

equations that pretend to work. We will find the children and see why there are these equations."

The mass of types shrilled their agreement and 8 grew and wavered in front of the types, preparing to speak. "We will stay to keep site open for return and we will watch for signs of your passage and will compulse if needed."

3 remained still through all the excitement of preparation for this exploration of their world. He stayed close to Bella and +. Gradually, all the other types became motionless in anticipation. Only *therefore* moved around, the three dots hardly able to stay still and incapable of staying together. Bella, kneeling now, concentrated on their activity to keep her imagination off whatever it was that was going to happen. 3 stretched his upper type towards her and Bella held it. Warmth radiated through it and the touch was shiny and smooth, like a crisp, ripe apple. Nothing was happening though, except now there was a movement in front of her eyes, a black dot buzzing back and forth so fast it became a blur. Suddenly, it dropped beside her. She looked down and three flat specks lay there. She thought of *therefore,* and wondered what he was doing. As she watched, the dots floated up and went slowly down again as if being boiled. But it was the light surrounding them that made her look around. Hues of red filled the space they were in, coming together every now and then to explode into white light. It was difficult to recognize the shapes that moved in this light but it seemed very busy and none of them was a mathematical form. Bella looked at 3. He had done it. They had compulsed to somewhere else.

Tony and Cassie

To Cassie's great relief, the terrible motion stopped. She waited, willing the world to stay still and hoping her need to vomit would go away. Nothing else happened. Flashes of light were intruding on her vision despite her closed eyes and it didn't help to relieve her nausea. She had to be sick. Darting for the direction of the door and the bathroom, she ran into an obstacle. She didn't feel a jolt or pain from the collision and assumed it was Tony. She vomited. Pushing feebly at the obstruction, she tried to shout around the saliva in her mouth.

"Tony, move away or get up. There is a mess here". The obstruction stayed. "What is wrong with you," she complained.

"Cassie, where are you? What is the problem?" Tony's voice came from another direction.

She opened her eyes. The lights must have gone out. There was only a torch beam...she shut her eyes again. Opening them, the torch beam remained and its light was coming from her eyes. She blinked a few times but nothing changed. It was black everywhere and the light beam briefly lit up all directions as Cassie, in alarm, rapidly searched for Tony. Flashes of colour distorted the light and confused her even more. She glimpsed him and had to concentrate so her eyelight would catch him. He was standing beside another boy and they were both flaring with different colours. The other boy was sitting at what appeared to be a desk and peering intently in front of him. Cassie could not understand what had his attention as she could clearly see his face and it was vacant with the intensity of looking.

"Come and look at this, Cassie." Tony waved his arm at her, encouraging her but also looking into the same empty space. They looked creepy, like a madness, and Cassie wondered whose it was.

She inspected her surroundings to see what sort of lunacy they were in. Colors, brilliant colors...just like those on the fireworks site...burst around her. They were not as irritating now she was feeling better. She looked down at her vomit or she supposed that's what it was. Congealing rapidly, it changed from a bilious yellow to the yellow of sunflowers. Its form changed as well so now it looked like a small pile of worms. Crimson dots appeared that leaked streaks through the now very bright yellow. Orange and green hues seem to fold the pile making it smaller until it disappeared. A deep blue light bathed her and slowly moved away. It was like slow motion and she noticed other colours also slow down mid flash. The nature of the flashes changed as well, creating strange silhouettes. Cassie moved her eyelight round what she supposed was a room. It felt like a room though she could not be sure she could see any walls. She thought it was best to go to Tony.

The space she had to cross was black. She could only see where she was going if she concentrated. Where she wanted to put her feet was always illuminated if she was looking down, but then she would lose sight of Tony. She focused her eyes on Tony and the boy and started towards them hoping there will be nothing to stumble over. The darkness was beside and behind her and it felt as if it were hiding something. She turned her head suddenly to catch the darkness unawares, nearly knocking herself off balance, but there was only the beam of light. Feeling foolish but grateful nothing did show itself, she reached a darker shadow in the shape of a desk and stood opposite the two boys. Even with her there, they were not distracted from the empty space in front of them.

"What is it that is so absorbing?" she demanded.

Tony looked up but leaned to the side and only then did he react to her presence.

"You won't see anything there, Cassie. Stand next to me."

She shrugged and went to him, casting her eyes in the general direction of their gaze. To her astonishment, she was looking at what could be a computer screen, except there was no screen. The images moved around freely in front of her but seemed to confine themselves to a prescribed space. Sometimes part of an image would go beyond the limit. It would stay there, hovering, until it was wanted and then it would be sucked back in. If not required, it would drift away.

The boy controlled how the images were displayed by using touch, some sort of remote device and vocal instructions. He was presently despairing of his own ingenuity and the images were splitting regretfully, some spilling out of the rectangle. Cassie moved to the opposite side of the table, careful not to bump into it even though the table didn't look solid, more like an impression of itself. Still, she could see nothing of the images or any kind of screen that would hide or contain them, only the concentration of the boy and the delighted face of Tony.

"How can the images be there like that, just free in the air?" she asked when she stood beside them again.

Tony looked at her in surprise. "He controls them of course. If he moved over there," Tony pointed into the dark, "as soon as he looked, it would be there."

He hadn't answered her question but Cassie thought maybe nobody could. It was just what this world did. The images were astounding. They looked alive, as if the boy was working with living things. "Are they his? Can we work them?"

Tony's attention was wandering around the darkness. "Only if he wants us to. But there is no need to ask him because mine will be over there. That is a good place. C'mon." He strolled over to a specific place in the darkness.

"'Bye," she said before following Tony. There was no response but Cassie was transfixed by a luminous green pillar that was reaching away from the concentration of images. Small implosions bisected its length, its upper part writhing as if in pain. Finally, the extra length broke free, landing on the floor and slowly crawled away. Cassie wasn't able to follow where it went while also keeping an eye on Tony and soon she lost it in the darkness.

"Look at this," exclaimed Tony.

His enthusiasm was for the images, his own images, Cassie supposed. He wasn't at all interested in the place they had both fallen into. Tony found everything astonishing but he hadn't wondered at how weird it all was. Cassie would rather look around to see what sort of place this was, but obediently she looked at the images in front of Tony and they were comfortably familiar. The design and placement of reference points were like his computer back home, more so somehow. It was solely for fireworks and already he was adding more relevant data and images. Then an engine appeared.

"What is an engine doing on a fireworks site?" asked Cassie.

"It is a noise distorter," Tony patiently instructed.

"How did it come up on the screen? Did you search for it? How did you know it even existed?"

"I don't need to search. I just imagined it and it appeared."

Cassie looked at Tony but he was immersed in his ideas as they came to life. She raised her voice. "How do you know all this? How did you know your screen was here? What is it you are doing here?"

Tony looked at her briefly with irritation. "I received some information and the rest I figured out myself."

"What do you mean figured out? From what? We have only been here a short time. That boy would not have been able to explain all that so quickly." Cassie remembered the boy sitting in silence and staring, only his fingers moving as he adjusted his images. "I don't think he could say that much in a year."

Now Tony looked at her with softer eyes. "But Cassie, we have been here for ages."

She stared at him. "No we haven't." She wanted to plead with him to realize they had only just arrived and to say something about how weird it all was. He didn't, so she had to continue. "But it doesn't matter how long we have been here because Mum and Dad will be worried already."

Tony was working his images, his attention again being taken away from Cassie and her concerns, but he did reply and his tone was abrupt. "They think we are doing our homework so they won't disturb us."

Cassie moved closer, trying to impress upon him the urgency of the matter.

"Dad may not disturb us but Mum notices things. She will worry and come up to your room."

"Aw Cassie, Mum worries too much."

Cassie clenched her fists in frustration. "But we won't be there Tony. Surely she can worry about that."

Tony was staring at her with a small smile on his face. "You sound just like Mum." He turned back to his images, talking aloud to himself as he experimented. "The time lapse is still mostly due to the speed of sound. Hmm…so what if the engine does produce a lapse…." Tony was absorbed and Cassie was left standing there, feeling stranded.

She was beginning to realize just how alone she was. She let her eyes stray, lighting the space piece by piece. There were others here, all boys as far as she could make out without obviously staring at them. She needn't have worried about the social graces though since they all appeared to be hypnotized by whatever images they were controlling. There was no chatter, the others hardly existed for any of them. They were alone as well but she was the only one without images. Plenty of imagery was firing around her and it demanded her attention in its boldness of colour and form. Just as she was beginning to comprehend one representation it would disperse. It was teasing her and she found she was eagerly waiting for the next transformation. The images appeared to be connected to pyrotechnics somehow. There were some that didn't have any connection, like the visual representation of music that was floating around the whole space, moving in and out of the other more explosive images. But as with Tony's engine, maybe she just didn't have the knowledge to connect it.

Cassie wondered where the images were coming from. Maybe they were fragments of ideas from the boys. She came to this conclusion after seeing what looked like Tony's engine sneak out of a crimson flash and move stealthily towards a cloud of orange. She thought they may be interacting somehow. After all, that is how ideas grow and the boys were not verbally sharing their ideas. She wondered if the boys were aware their ideas might be meeting others. She hoped they were. It seemed healthy which took away some of the concern she felt at seeing the boys so intent on their own small spaces, not even wanting to look at where they were or who else was with them. She watched the floating images and thought she was being fanciful...but they were a brilliant kaleidoscope of knowledge and adventure and the mingling or abruptly moving away did seem to have intent. The bursts of eccentric colours didn't help in the comprehension. The light bathed everything, seeming to change the dimensions of the ideas so she would lose them. Except for a slithering mass that had just fallen away from one of the boys' images. As it hit the ground it lay still and then straightened up, stopping at about three feet high. In her eyelight it seemed to preen itself. She had no doubt it was some sort of creature. There was space around it, no images intruded. It glistened in Cassie's eyelight, its shape distorted by peristaltic action. Dark spots appeared here and there. The shape was still again before it slowly revolved. Finally it stopped. The dark spots looked sinister now as Cassie could see into them, murky depths that seemed too big for the size of the creature. It was mesmerizing but she had to pull away, shutting her eyes. Slowly she opened them again. The creature was gone. She looked up at the boy from whose images it had crawled. Tony! What was he doing with such a horrible thing? A low reverberating blast shattered a purple cloud near Cassie's head. She instinctively ducked, but nothing fell onto her. One of the boys was putting his fist into the air and even seemed to be showing emotion. It was only a brief moment as now he was busy again and a loud crack filled the space. Cassie again bowed her head and shoulders, to straighten quickly, feeling foolish as no one else showed any reaction.

Nobody, so far, had taken any notice of her. Certainly not the boys. She wondered about the authority that would appear to check on them, make sure they were doing the right thing. Like her mum, who always seemed in a state of worry over their well being though she pretended only a casual concern. Would the authority here be kind and supportive if it did enter? She looked around. The ideas and colours continued to heave around her, erratic and unruly, especially when compared to the pale faces of the boys. All their blood seemed to have been absorbed by their images. Despite their pale complexions, the boys didn't seem to need any support at all, they had everything they required. And whoever was giving it to them knew how to keep them captivated. Conversation did not appear to be encouraged or even necessary here, but Cassie felt she had to find out what sort of place this was and who was in charge of the rules. She wanted to know before any authority did notice her. Talking to Tony wouldn't be helpful now. He would dismiss her questions as worry or of no concern of hers because he knew what he was doing and had everything under control. She would have to try and engage the other boys in conversation. She studied them. There were only three others besides Tony, but as her eyes lit up areas in the space, another one appeared. His presence startled Cassie as she was sure she had carefully scanned that particular area. Working methodically, she had let her eyes rest on and light up one piece of space after another. Now, here was someone who had been there in the dark all the time. Unless of course he had only just arrived. The boy's sudden presence made her nervous, which conversely, decided for her whom to approach.

Cassie kept her eyes on him, not trusting that she would find him again if she looked away. He was smaller than the others, probably only Cassie's age. She stood beside him, not wanting to look over his shoulder at his images until she was asked. Now she stressed over what to say that would break his intense concentration and would be interesting enough to keep his attention. The boy relieved her of that challenge.

"I have never seen a girl here before," he stated without looking at her.

"How long has that been?" asked Cassie.

"Forever." He still had not taken his eyes from his images.

Cassie hoped he wasn't speaking literally. "That is a long time." At the risk of sounding flippant she continued, "Were you born here?"

Now he looked at her. "Does it matter?"

Cassie thought about that. "I suppose it depends on what you do here."

He pointed to his images. "You can look if you want but you will not understand."

Cassie was quite ready to believe that and realized she was a bit nervous about looking at his images. What if the images are a reflection of what is in their minds? She didn't know if she wanted that much information. She moved to the back of him and looked up. Well, she thought, if that is his mind he is beautifully creative. The colours were bright and cheerful and the images moved to a rapid beat. Then she heard a low hum that became a slow melody. It sounded sad, which contradicted the brilliant colours that streaked away in improbable lines to meet briefly, forming a new entity, only to break away in search of other forms.

"What does it mean...apart from being beautiful?"

"Does it need another function?" The boy sounded angry.

"No, I suppose it doesn't," Cassie conceded.

"Well, it does have another purpose anyway. But there is no reason why it should not be beautiful as well."

Cassie waited but she had to prompt him again. "So, what does it do?"

"I am trying to create a mechanism that allows choice in direction during the line of flight of a force-propelled object."

"These are fireworks aren't they?" Cassie wanted to be sure in her assumption that the space they were in concentrated on one subject only.

"Of course it is, but the knowledge can be useful for ideas

elsewhere."

"Useful to other boys here or other places?" Cassie asked.

"I don't know but after one of my ideas, I was contacted and my images were shared."

"Contacted?... How?" But Cassie had been too abrupt and maybe too interested. The boy was looking at her again. "Don't you have your own images?"

Cassie returned his stare, then sat down on the floor beside him, not knowing from where or even how to get a chair.

"No, but I am getting one," she said, trying to sound part of the set-up.

"You do not get images. They are here waiting for you," the boy explained in a stern voice.

"Well, I came with my brother so there may be some confusion over providing two at once."

He was still watching her, but now looked undecided. "That could happen. Two have never arrived together before." He seemed to be trying to remember something.

Cassie took advantage of this hesitancy to start again. "My name is Cassie. I am pleased to meet you."

"Um," he seemed undecided, then became stern again. "My name is Michael. Not Mike or Mickey, Michael only."

"Of course, Michael. Shortening names can be annoying. Though my name is really Cassandra and I am pleased to have it shortened."

Michael looked confused so Cassie kept going. "The music playing in your images is very beautiful. What is it?"

"I made it. Every image, whether it is visual, auditory or sensual, we make ourselves." He was talking like a teacher and Cassie thought it best to keep the conversation on Michael personally to keep his mind off her own lack of images and purpose in this place.

"Your music has a lovely sound. Have you written more?"

"The sound is only background support for the more important image of movement." He turned back to his images.

She was being rebuffed, though Michael was truly forgetting

her presence as he immersed himself in his ideas. What is it about these images? Cassie thought angrily, everyone was fixated on them. They are the only interest these boys have, so to make friends here, she has to show enthusiasm for their ideas.

"Can you fully control the movement of the fireworks?" she asked with determined interest.

Michael sighed, just as Tony does when he is working on something far too important to be interrupted, especially by someone who wouldn't understand it anyway. But like Tony, Michael couldn't resist showing off his knowledge.

"No. Not yet. There are lots of ways flight can be influenced, propulsion, the outer covering and the shedding of it, size and shape of course and even the noise the fireworks make. Understand these and others and mix them in the right proportions and you can plot many directional courses for the firework." He looked at her. "It is very complicated but very exciting."

"It would be," Cassie agreed, especially as while Michael had been talking and gesticulating, the images on the screen were reflecting his enthusiasm. She had listened and watched avidly. Swirls, streaks and balls had fled across his space, sometimes to stop suddenly and explode, other times to hesitate, try a couple of directions before flaring away somewhere unexpected. Others fell where they started and one ball of fire escaped from the image space completely and rolled across the floor. All the time the slow melodies were playing, ignoring the rapturous movements its beat was supposed to accompany.

"And when you can control the direction, is it your creation? Do you own, what is the word, the pattern?"

"The patent," Michael corrected. "I don't know. The excitement is in the discovery."

Cassie thought about this. For all his creativity, Michael is still only a small boy. She looked again at his images.

"I look forward to seeing a fireworks display that has your creations."

Michael was quiet for a while. "Yes, that would be fun. I want to be qualified to be able to hold firework displays."

"Where would you hold the displays?" Cassie asked.

Michael shifted in his seat but didn't look at her. "Maybe instead, I will want to keep inventing better ones," he insisted.

Cassie could hear the tension in his voice and it sounded unsure. She wondered if he thought he could be somewhere other than in this place. She backed away from creating more uncertainty.

"Where are the fireworks you have invented? Do you have a record of them?"

"No, I remember them. They are all up here." He tapped his head.

"And the ones you have shared? What happened to them?"

Michael leaned closer to Cassie. "I do not know how they have been used. They have been sent out to help others, just like sometimes I receive images that help me." He sat back. "Your brother sends me images of noise variations which I can use."

Cassie was impressed. "Already, gosh, he is moving ahead with his knowledge. Do you have brothers that you share things with?"

Michael looked confused. "Brothers? No. Nobody helped." He stopped. "I had a friend once, but we…." He suddenly turned to his image space. "Oh, look at that!"

There was that order again, thought Cassie, but she did look. It was a text, as far as she could make out, explaining the latest about zinc and clouds. Michael was enraptured.

"That could also help shift…where are my chemical equations." He was talking to himself as he moved his fingers over the space and tapped the desk. The images moved as rapidly as his thoughts. Cassie had been forgotten as had his friend.

She sat back in the darkness beside Michael's chair to figure out what she had learnt from their conversation. Nothing much, she thought despondently. But then she doesn't know what there is to find out, so if she takes the time to think, she may realize she has discovered a lot. First of all, Michael is very enthusiastic about his knowledge and the topic of fireworks. He is also allowed to develop his knowledge in any way he wants.

There are no restrictions put on his searches. They are even helped by having other relevant information passed onto him. The enthusiasm is for the development of his knowledge and abilities. But he doesn't know what happens to any achievement and he certainly doesn't have control over where his work goes. He has a past, or at least memories that do not belong to his life in front of the images. There was uncertainty about them though and Cassie wondered why. Is it because he can't remember clearly, or is he not allowed to remember? She sat up. Where did the last thought come from? When he was remembering his friend, his thoughts were interrupted by something on the images that caught his attention. But he controls the images so how could anything surprise him so completely? It must have been a shared image. Somebody sent him a distraction just at the right time. No, thought Cassie. It must be a coincidence. Otherwise…otherwise there would be intent, some sort of control over Michael and his ideas.

The only thing outside the images Michael took note of was that Cassie didn't have her own. He could hardly comprehend being here without images, and Cassie, without them, was standing out as abnormal. She tried to not be worried by this thought. She let her eyes cast light around the space again and still it was only the images and the boys intently creating them. Wait! She returned her vision to one of the boys. What was he doing? She realized, with surprise, he was eating a hamburger and a large helping of fries and still his stare remained on the images. She wondered where the food had come from. She didn't notice anyone arriving with it and certainly no microwave or food facility was here. Then she wondered where it would go eventually. She hadn't felt hungry or thirsty since arriving here, even after vomiting. After watching the transformation of the vomit, the destruction of other matter would be interesting,…maybe.

Cassie approached the boy, his hands hardly sparing the time from creating to shovel food into his mouth.

"Hi," greeted Cassie once she was beside him. There was no reply. She studied the nearly finished hamburger and fries. The

half-eaten hamburger bun looked fresh as did the enclosed sal-
ads. The fries also looked delicious, crisp, golden brown and
thick with creamy potato inside. Very like all the advertised pictures of hamburgers and fries but never reproduced in the actual food. Leaning closer, she thought she could detect a tantaliz-
ing odour even though it must be cool by now. She reached out
to feel for any heat.

"Have a fry if you want."

Cassie quickly withdrew her hand. She had forgotten it was
someone else's food. Recovering though, she took a fry.
"Thanks." It was warm and solid in her fingers but it didn't taste
like anything. She even wondered if she had dropped it and
looked down at her feet.

"Good fries," she exclaimed. "Where did they come from?"

"The local place. They are always good."

"How did you order them?"

"They are always there when you want to eat."

He was being friendly though he hadn't taken his eyes off his
images. Cassie was getting used to this way of conversing, talking to the side of a face.

"So, where are the toilets here?"

"Over there probably." He waved his arm in a vague direction which caused one of the images to suddenly veer away and
fall off the space before the boy could recover it.

Cassie watched the fallen image on the floor. It rolled briefly
before coming to a stop. Then it unfolded itself and ran away.
Cassie bent to look closer. It was about six inches tall and ran
jerkily, every now and then, leaping into the air. It didn't seem
to be able to coordinate its legs. Cassie tried to count them but
it was moving very awkwardly, three legs at least, and the whole
creature was different shades of red. It looked contagious she
thought, straightening up and hoping it would disappear soon.
Suddenly, it stopped and looked directly at her. It had a very
creased face, even more so now as it was showing its teeth. Its
eyes bulged through the creases and retreated again. Cassie
could see all this very clearly because not only was it in her eye

light but it seemed to be generating its own glow. Unknowingly, she moved closer to the boy. The creature was making her uncomfortable. Then it raised one of its limbs, pointed it at her and suddenly, it wasn't in her eye light. Now it could be anywhere and Cassie wasn't sure if that was worse.

She looked at the images in the boy's space. He was still rapt in them and the fries had gone. As had the wrappings and the area was clean. She couldn't understand any of this or the meaning of the boy's ideas.

"What are you making? My name is Cassie, by the way."

"Douglas. Other ways for fireworks to explode."

"What do you mean?"

"Just mucking around mixing substances, seeing what happens." Cassie was quiet and he continued. "The explosive elements in a firework need to be stabilized. This can affect the brilliance of the color, its visual effect and trajectory. I am experimenting with gases and their ratios to see what else can work. Reinventing gunpowder, I hope."

Cassie was surprised at his eloquence. She had the impression of mindlessness. But she should not have prejudged because her first introduction to some of Tony's friends had been to their backs as they sat immersed in their computers. She hadn't recognized them when she had met them at school with their intelligent conversation and sharp wits.

"Where do you go to school?" The question was an extension of her thoughts.

"I don't bother with that."

"Well, where do you go when you do bother to go?"

For the first time he looked at her and it was only for a moment. He could be older than Tony, she thought, probably didn't go to school anymore.

"I don't go anywhere," he said.

"But before you came here, where were you?"

He was looking at his images again but would turn his attention to Cassie now and then. "Home, I suppose, but I left it."

"And if you wanted to go back...." Cassie faltered. She hadn't thought of home for a while. Too busy trying to find out about this place. How would they leave here? Douglas glanced at her.

"Which exit would you take?" she continued illogically.

He smiled. "There are many."

"Which exit here? Where is the door to outside?"

"I don't know and it doesn't matter much. I have my work to do here." So saying, he leaned closer towards his images, absently picking up the half-liter Coke sitting on the side. It looked cold as condensation bubbled along the sides of the container. But it hadn't left a ring of moisture where it had been standing.

Cassie was discouraged. She was learning nothing that would help to return them home. The boys were so intent on their work they didn't notice anything else. She thought it was very odd here, and remembering the little creatures, she felt she should be afraid as well, but no one else seemed to think so. They were content here. She suddenly missed Tony. The picture of him not being here flashed through her mind. She hadn't seen him for a long time. She desperately cast her eyes around the space but Tony didn't appear in any of the lighted areas. She wanted to run and shout his name but was shackled by the darkness that surrounded her. She made herself stand still and methodically scan the space. She also had to resist the rising panic so she could properly search where her vision cast light. There, that surely was him. There was the familiar hunched back and he was laughing. Now and then he threw his head back and she could tell he was laughing even though she couldn't hear him. Concentrating on keeping Tony in her eyelight, she walked towards him. Finally she stood near him and with relief, she put her hand on his back.

"Hi, Tony."

"Cassie, I was wondering where you were."

Tony had taken his eyes from his images and was smiling at her. But only for a brief second. He was looking at the images as he continued the conversation.

"This is a great set-up," Tony enthused. "It seems to know

how I want my engine to work and a couple of times I didn't even have to make the suggestion."

Cassie listened carefully. His chatter was a release for his abundant enthusiasm and could sound like an incoherent ramble.

"Sometimes it does happen too quickly and I have to think about what has just been changed but at least this prevents irrelevant connections so I am not wasting time looking. It is fun. I have to stay alert as the images have momentum and the next step forward is very close and it requires concentration to guide the images in the direction you want before it goes somewhere that is not in the plan or design." He stopped talking to move his fingers over the images and tap the desk in front of him.

"There now, look at that. It won't work. The sound may speed up but the benefit has been lost elsewhere because of the fluid. Just let me figure out these calculations again."

Cassie was thinking that this conversation was actually no different from those with the other boys. But Tony was her brother, she didn't have to be subtle, she could even get angry with him if he tried to ignore her.

"What are you trying to do, Tony?"

"Sound, Cassie. Trying to delay or even stop it. There is already the Salute where you see the firework and hear the bang. But that relies on the rapidity of the flash powder to keep ahead of the sound. I want to delay the sound. You could even harmonize the effect. And what if the sound came from a different direction altogether? You wouldn't know where to look."

Cassie caught his enthusiasm. They had laughed so often at their wild imaginings of how fireworks could behave. Now it seemed Tony believed he could make them real. She remembered the other boys and their ideas, one trying to control the line of flight and the other creating different ways for the fireworks to explode. What a show they could put on eventually. They must be helping each other with information. Didn't one say Tony had sent him something helpful?

"Between the three of you, no wonder you are moving along so fast. And there are the other two boys I haven't met yet. I wonder how they are contributing?"

"What other boys? What do you mean?" Tony was sounding impatient but it may be because his images are playing up as his eyes were focused there.

Cassie slowly moved her eyes around the space. Light picked out young Michael and one other she hadn't spoken to yet.

"The other boys," she explained. "They are working on fireworks too. One said he received information from you that helped him."

"Well, it is good it has helped but I didn't send it. Sometimes I receive information. It may come from them, but I haven't sent any. I do not know what they are doing so I do not know what is relevant for them."

"But you must do," insisted Cassie, "otherwise who is giving them information? Who is helping you in your research?"

"Cassie, what are you going on about? I have my images here and I am finding out things by working them. Nobody is helping except that information is being accumulated. I am downloading anything I need."

Cassie was getting angry with him. She balled her hands into fists because she wanted to thump him, wanted to make him look around, to share the oddness of this place with her.

"And is it all there? Is there any bit of information you need that has not slipped into your images? Have you needed food? Are you hungry yet?" She stopped, knowing she sounded hysterical but still glared at Tony because what she said was true. They aren't hungry here. They aren't anything that is normal back home. It was only an hour or so before bedtime when they found themselves here and she hadn't even yawned and Tony was not looking sleepy.

He was staring at her. "You have never found fireworks interesting. You were always more concerned about their effect on dogs and other animals. But that doesn't mean I cannot have fun with them." He turned his back on her, returning to the progress of his ideas.

Cassie stepped back, confused by the sneering tone in his

voice. Tony had never before talked to her like that. He was shoving her aside as selfish and uncaring of his needs. She couldn't understand what was happening to them and she felt like crying. She wondered how useful this would be. Tears would be a relief but she would still have to drag herself out of the hurt and nobody here would even notice let alone care about her tears. Best to use the effort for crying to stop the tears before they started. Anyway, even if it were true what Tony said, it still didn't change their situation. They were here and she wanted to be home but she didn't know how to get back there. She thought of what Tony said. Maybe he didn't want to go home. No…that was silly. But even if he didn't, he would want to know how to get there when he did. She continued to stand there, hesitating before this brother who wanted to hurt her with his words.

She blurted out, "I want to go home and I am going to find out how to get there."

There was silence from Tony as he concentrated on his images. Finally he spoke.

"You do that."

Cassie waited for more and he did continue but without looking at her. "I will join you when I am ready."

She glared at him, even though he wasn't looking at her. He can be such an idiot, Cassie thought, as she walked away.

Right, she thought, now to find a way home. Immediately she felt discouraged because she would have to talk to these unresponsive boys again. It was hard work. The alternative was to look for anything that might help, like a door. She walked past Tony into an area she thought she hadn't explored yet, though it was difficult to tell. She was ill at ease in doing so and stopped every couple of steps to pick up Tony in her eyelight. It would be much easier if the space was flooded with light, but she was restricted to the narrow beam of light her eyes created. Searching for anything was a slow process and she certainly didn't want to stumble over any of those hideous things that kept falling out of the boys' images. The continual flashes of color were also a distraction and things looked distorted in it. Maybe, she thought, that is why sometimes the boys are not where she expects them to be.

"I can order you your own burger if you want."

Cassie looked behind her and found she was standing next to Douglas. She didn't bother to try and figure it out. Maybe she was getting used to this place.

"Thank you, but I am not hungry." That was true anyway.

"You're never hungry here," replied the boy.

Cassie didn't know how to take this. Either he was supplied with food all the time or he knew he wasn't ever hungry here. She was thinking too much. She should just ask the questions she wants the answers to.

"Where is here?" she asked.

He turned his chair to face her. Cassie was taken aback at this confrontation. To be able to break away from the enchantment of the images had seemed to be an impossible thing to do.

"Haven't you guessed? But the more intriguing question is why you are not absorbed in your own images or at least pretending to be. Wandering around declaring yourself lost as you have been doing is a dangerous activity. Hang on a minute."

He turned back to his images. His fingers crossed and zigzagged over his space. The images flared, decreased to redundant points but some exploded again. Cassie watched closely and she thought she could see creatures, their outlines pale in the background and they seemed to be creating their own chaos whenever they happened to entangle with an image. She wondered if controlling their actions was also part of whatever it was Douglas was planning. She looked closer…one looked like the thing she had seen fall from Tony's space. She was pushed back.

"Careful," Douglas said. He was looking at her again. "You really do not know this place, do you?"

He was annoying her with his patronizing attitude so she put aside her common sense. She could only say what it felt like, not what made any sense.

"It is some sort of computer world," she replied.

"Well done. And it is your brother who has a fascination with pyrotechnics and he was attracted by a certain site and you were with him for whatever reason and became caught up with him when he was brought here."

She regarded his smiling face with suspicion. "How did you know?"

"I have been here for quite some time and have managed to see some of what this world is doing."

"So what is it doing?"

"It is encouraging invention," Douglas stated.

Cassie wasn't prepared for an answer that supported this world. It was too weird, and she could feel menace here. "It can do this by kidnapping people?"

"Look at your brother," said Douglas, nodding in a direction, "does he think he is here against his will?"

Cassie held her fists to her side. She was frustrated with his reasoning and wanted to thump him like she feels she needs to do now and then with Tony. Instead she stamped her foot which she regretted as she saw Douglas smile at her.

"But it isn't right," she finally answered.

Douglas shrugged and worked at his images for a few minutes before turning his attention back to Cassie. She was still trying to formulate an explanation of why this place wasn't right but could only go back to what she really wanted to do.

"Is there a way home? If everyone is not here forcibly, there must be a way to leave even if for a short time."

"Well, Cassie. I am sure there is for Tony. You may be more difficult as I don't think you are supposed to be here."

She stared at him...but she was here and she wasn't going to stay. And why should it be more difficult for her? "The images...," she murmured as she thought about how they had travelled to here. "We can go back through the images. How does that work?"

Douglas reluctantly faced Cassie again. "I am not quite sure. If you can find a link between two places, you can get transported to the other place."

"I don't understand," said Cassie, "what would a link be?"

"It is like a common strand or connecting facts that run through two places or sites. Concentrate on that and somehow you turn up on the other site."

"But I don't want to go to another site, I want to get to the outside, to the street where our house is."

Douglas was silent for a while.

"You will just have to find a connection between here and your street then."

Cassie folded her arms across her chest. "That is all you can come up with? You said you had been to other places here and also that Tony could get home. You must know something about how this place connects to the outside."

Douglas frowned at her. "I do know. I am, after all, the one who has been here the longest. I just haven't properly thought about it. Let me think now." He turned back to his images and fiddled there for a few minutes. Cassie was becoming impatient with this absorption in the images.

"I think the images prevent you from thinking," she declared, trying to interrupt his concentration. Douglas became still and slowly turned to face her again. He was looking serious now.

"They do, but only if you let them. First, you have to begin to realize that they are taking other thoughts away from you. Not many of the boys I have seen know that much." He was talking with much more enthusiasm. "Once you understand that, there is still the continual struggle to be aware of how the images are manipulating you. Then you have to stay ahead of them, a difficult task made more so, as you have to do it without them knowing what you are up to."

Cassie was silent, her arms relaxed at her sides, trying to follow his words. "You are talking as if all this is under somebody's control. That this somebody is making all these boys do what it wants to do."

Douglas was nodding his head. "Yes, that is what I am saying. I haven't really expressed it before as there was no reason to. I have been to other sites. They are challenging and fun.

Well they would be because that particular site holds interest for you and it supplies all the information you want and by exploring and experimenting you can keep finding more." He focused on her now. "When you have discovered something that may have more relevance at another site and persist with it, that is when you move to other sites." He looked away.

"So you can move around this world through information?"

Douglas worked his images for a bit, but Cassie could now see the alertness in his face was only when he was talking, trying to explain this world. "Yes. But the kids here don't realize that. I don't think some of them even know they have moved to another site. They are just doing what everyone does at sites, explore their ideas further and further so it is difficult to draw away and then they don't even bother to try. When they do go from site to site, they are not conscious of it. For them, it is just more information and bigger challenges for their skills."

"But they could leave here if they wanted to?"

Douglas was fidgeting, his hands giving away his uneasiness, usually not apparent when they were working the images. He looked into the blackness beside Cassie. "I am not sure they can. They have to know they can and want to. That way of thinking has been gradually deleted from their minds."

Cassie clasped her hands together as she searched the space for the boys. Ominously, her eyelight couldn't find them and she was beginning to understand. The world of the boys narrowed to the progress they made with their images. There was nothing else here: no dogs or trees, no breezes or laughter to be carried on it. Even music was silent. Michael, who could make beautiful music, didn't know he could because of the immediate challenge of his images. Her eyelight had picked out one of the boys she hadn't met yet. He was hunched over his images but she couldn't see them as he was facing her. Or would be if he looked up. All she could see was the intense watchfulness on his face. He looked as if life had been taken out of him.

"Do you boys talk about things?" asked Cassie. "I mean, are they curious about where they are?"

"Did Tony show any curiosity when he came?"

Cassie slowly shook her head as she tried to locate him. There he was and if she hadn't known him so well, she would have found it difficult to note any difference between him and the other boy. She wondered how she could be in more danger than these lifeless boys.

"They have their images," remarked Douglas, as if reading her mind. "They belong here. You don't."

"What is it I have to be worried about?" Cassie asked. She thought maybe she wouldn't be as scared if she knew what she was up against, especially if it explained the creatures she saw. Douglas however, made her more anxious when he swung back to his images and busied himself.

"I don't know," he finally replied. He kept his back to her. "There was one site I progressed to that was very difficult." He turned to her, smiling. "Nothing that I couldn't handle of course, but...." He fell quiet, his smile disappearing. "The images were hard to control and the information wasn't quite what I wanted. For one thing, it was working with equations much bigger than I needed and therefore could change the whole purpose of my ideas." His smiling bravado returned. "I had to fight the images and the progress they wanted to make. Eventually it became easier and I realized I was at another and more familiar site. But the other site had felt dangerous somehow. I wondered what would have happened to me if my ideas did move out of my realm of understanding."

Cassie thought about this. "But staying here will not get me home. I will have to risk going somewhere else."

"Well, you should leave the way you came, with your brother. His images will be familiar and therefore control will be easier."

Now Cassie was worried. "You mean I have to convince him to go home," her voice was rising, "get him to find the sites that will lead us there?"

"Yes," said Douglas. "I will talk to him as well, he is doing awesome stuff with sound."

This wasn't quite the type of cooperation Cassie wanted, but it was a start she supposed. Douglas was walking with assurance towards Tony. Cassie concentrated on keeping her eyelight on Douglas's back as she followed closely.

"Douglas?"

"What?" he replied without slowing down.

"Is your vision like a torch beam?"

"I can see okay. Oh…yes, light is only where you are looking. You soon get used to it. After all, what is there to look at except the images?"

Tony didn't look up at their approach. Cassie wondered if he even knew they were there despite his exclamation, "Look at this!" Maybe he just shouts that at regular intervals.

Douglas immediately sat in a chair beside him. Cassie could only stare at the chair's presence. She looked around for another one. There wasn't one. She tried assuming a chair would appear but only fell onto the floor. Getting up, she leant over the shoulders of Tony and Douglas. Both were working the images though there wasn't any chatter between them. Cassie watched the images but couldn't find any association with home. How could there be, she thought, the images were of sound, its speed, vibrations and projections. It is a long way from Tony's untidy bedroom. It was also boring as they were not exchanging information or even arguing with each other.

She looked into the surrounding darkness. Michael was over there, a long way off yes, but she couldn't seem to keep her eyelight on him. He kept moving even though he was sitting down. She might be unconsciously moving her head. She kept her head still but her eyes started watering with the strain of keeping Michael in focus. Blinking, she caught the shape of another boy. No…it wasn't a boy, it looked like that horrible creature with the dark spots. Its legs jerked about and she was looking at one of the boys again. Her eyelight was moving away from the boy and there was that creature again. It was sitting now, creasing its pulpy face, one of the dark spots she could see was a mouth and it was getting bigger. Cassie shut her eyes. She had an awful feeling it could trap her eyelight so it would forever be in her vision no matter where she looked. She turned back to Tony and Douglas, her fright making her sound demanding.

"Have you found any connection yet?"

Douglas was enthusiastic. "This is very clever. The sound could be blocked...."

"No, not blocked," interrupted Tony, "muffled by its own speed before being released."

"But you could create a block by delaying," insisted Douglas.

Cassie shouted above their eagerness. "Douglas, will it lead to a site closer to home?"

"Not yet, Cassie. But look, Tony, if you add more...."

"It won't work like that," Tony protested.

Their argument continued and Cassie was pleased to hear the sounds of a normal boy friendship again, but it was still a boring thing to listen to.

She wondered if she would see the creature again or if it was all her imagination. She was conscious of the dark behind her and he could be there still, maybe getting closer. She wished she had her own images so she didn't have to think about this place. Nobody else seemed to be concerned about these odd creatures. Maybe they are harmless. She had to know if it was behind her. Quickly, she turned around, directing her eyelight onto the area immediately surrounding her. Nothing. What a relief. She turned back to Tony and Douglas. No one was there. She swung around looking for them and caught a glimpse of a glistening shape. Panic gripped her. She scanned in front of her again, between herself and the images. She tried to shout their names over the lump in her throat, but Tony and Douglas were not there anymore and their images were slowly fading away.

Bella

A jumble of images and words filled the spaces around Bella. They had substance, she realized, they were not one-dimensional at all but seemed to be living things. They moved continually, lit up intermittently with a fluorescent glow. None of them were avoiding Bella and her companions. The figures were unconcerned that she was standing, suddenly, in their midst. The images and information crowded her vision, but it was difficult to grasp any purpose as any form she was looking at would suddenly be replaced by another. It was as if she could only see everything out of the corner of her eye. 3 had done it alright, they had compulsed to somewhere else, she just wasn't sure to what or where. The connection between the woman, dressed in jeans and a cropped t-shirt, who surprised her by casting a friendly glance their way, and the hen that was now scratching round her feet was not immediately obvious. Darting forward, the hen pecked at Bella's foot. A dot flew up to her shoulder and she could see two others buzzing round the hen. *Therefore*! She was sure he wasn't supposed to be here with them but was not surprised he did manage to tag along. As she watched the procession of information, she felt grateful it wasn't to here she had first landed. She thought of the mathematical site with affection, a place that was apparent in its function. Here, she felt she would have readily accepted the idea of her insanity and kept her eyes closed until everything had disappeared. She glanced at 3. He and + were unmoving amongst the confusion. *Therefore* was now perched on top of 3, his dots separating for brief moments before returning to their vantage point. 3 shook himself causing them to fall off. Before the hen noticed, they quickly reassembled and went to Bella's shoulders for safety.

"We are somewhere else," said 3, somewhat in wonder.

"A successful compulse, 3, well done. But where do you think we are?" Bella asked.

"It looks familiar," mused 3.

+ stretched upwards. "Of course it is, it is all threes."

Bella looked around at the tumbling images and words. Ethereal beings passed by her. She counted them and they were in groups of 3. The woman in jeans and cropped t-shirt seemed to be with two others. Suddenly she was smiling again at Bella and she couldn't help smiling in return but the woman had already been replaced. It was a male, dressed in a business suit complete with the tie, the irrational symbol of formality. He rushed by but was still able to stare impatiently at them as if they were obstructing him in some way. The otherworldly substance of these beings brought theology to mind and Bella wondered about their personification. Whatever the lady represented, the world needed more of and the man brought to mind the three roots of evil of Buddhism. He could have been hate, greed or delusion though she supposed they overlapped anyway. Other images were claiming prominence. They came from stories – pigs, musketeers, bears. Still more information intruded and Bella had to concentrate to be able to recognize the familiar. It was not helped by the colored lights suffusing over everything before blending into a white light. It created a sensation of movement as if in a boat, unless, Bella wondered, the space was actually moving. The edges seemed to grow and decrease and as her mind adjusted to being in a small space, it protruded out-wards again. It was too much for any of her senses. She looked at 3, + and *therefore*, who was now only two dots with one lying flat on the ground. The other two were circling around it, only stopping to jump on it.

"Are you still functioning?" asked 3 of the two buzzing dots.

Their energy and mischief sapped anyone of the resolve to admonish *therefore* for following the compulse.

The two parts stopped the task of reviving (Bella assumed this was what they were doing) their other part, and replied with patience. "It is difficult as we cannot comprehend the consequence of all this. We are ineffectual. But," they resumed their stomping, "if we all stayed alert, maybe we would see what can happen."

+ wasn't concerned with *therefore*, he was assessing and counting their surroundings.

"Can you hear the triad? Look, the three witches and there is the soul."

Bella tried to remember what she knew of the soul and how she would picture it. Here it appeared as three swirls of vapour that blended together now and then and all the time forming any shape you wished upon them. "Plato described it, didn't he?"

"Divided it into three," answered 3, "the appetitive, the spiritual and the rational."

"So you are here in everything," Bella was lost in the surprise of it. "It is just a matter of knowing how."

"Even this space," continued +, "three spatial dimensions, length, width, height or depth. You can see it. Though it works only because it omits the fourth dimension, time. which...."

"Three dimensions are fine for now," interrupted Bella, who was experiencing information overload.

A white cube rolled past, its bottom edges flattening slightly with the movement.

"What is the three in that?" she asked, pointing.

3 looked to the cube. "Its atomic number. The cube is lithium."

Bella was being inundated with images and information. Just like, she realized, when she entered a topic in the computer and many varied connotations appeared. She always had an immediate sense of panic, thinking she would never find what she wanted in the overflow of information. But most times she did, plus a couple of interesting gems.

+ was murmuring, counting, Bella realized. It was his essence, she supposed, to add more. "Not three children," he remarked sadly.

"So what happens?" asked *therefore*. The two dots had propped up the recumbent one between them. They created a line that in literature, can be a questioning pause. This association in Bella's mind made them look broken. She wanted to help them.

"We need to find a connection from here to the children...therefore they will be." She faltered to a finish, pleased her companions were not from a grammatical site.

The line of dots stirred and suddenly formed their regular pattern.

"Have three angles again. We are consequential, therefore the children are here," they declared.

3 went close to *therefore*. "That is illogical. This compulse is not good for you. Do you want to go back?"

The three dots exploded away and from a distance and nearly in unison, shouted. "No! We want to search and we will try to become of no consequence to anything."

Bella couldn't help smiling. They were not making sense to her and she supposed for a mathematical equation, not making sense could be, eventually, ruinous. But maybe tenuous answers could be of some help here. Nothing really made sense and they were only making up the search as they went along.

3 was tapping her knee. "Let us look."

The colours flowed over everything, making it difficult to perceive where an image started and finished.

"Why do the colours circulate like that?" asked Bella.

"Three colours, red, green and blue are the primary hues that compose white light," 3 replied.

Bella noticed when she stopped to look, the images closest to her seemed to slow down so she could comprehend its meaning. But now, in front of her there was only two of something. She searched for the third but the image remained only two.

3 was beside her. "Gemini, the twins," he explained, "but the

third astrological sign."

A small flame appeared as if from a match. Bella pointed. "The flame?"

+ jumped around in front of Bella. "Bad luck comes in threes. This belief probably came from the trenches during the first world war. Lighting three cigarettes from the same match gave the enemy the opportunity to sight you, take aim and on the third cigarette, to fire."

Bella couldn't think of any connection with the children. There was so much information and none of it obvious for her needs. 3 sensed her confusion.

"This is a site for three. Look how much. Any of these will lead to more information. There will be something to connect to the children in any of them."

"You are right 3 and I have to decide." She wondered what fact would attract a teenage boy. It would have to be something associated with danger and probably useless. She felt sure that it was Tony who had dragged them all here. For some sort of inspiration she watched *therefore*. In his present state he mimicked Tony with the lack of awareness for consequences. *Therefore* was fully recovered and zipping round the space. They went through the ethereal figures, none paying any attention to the black things dissecting them. One dot was hurtling towards the cube of lithium. It didn't pass through but landed with a splat, disappeared in a little way and then slid slowly down the side and onto the floor. The other two dots carried it away. She turned to 3.

"What is lithium?"

"A soft metal. We can compulse there for more information."

Metal, Bella thought, something boys associate with all the time with their fascination for machines. Certainly more likely than the stories about the musketeers or witches which Bella would have enjoyed exploring. "Okay, lithium it is."

Bella waited for something to happen. Instead she heard + saying, as if from a long way, "No, not three, they are not three."

She tried to look down at + to see why he was so agitated

but realized she couldn't see anything and moving her head was difficult. Not that there was any pain or discomfort, her body just seemed content with its present posture. Before she could think properly about this, she heard 3 say quite clearly, "Back, we go back."

Finally, Bella could see again and it was still the site of three. They hadn't moved at all. "What happened?" she asked.

"*Therefore* was not ready."

Bella looked for the three dots but she couldn't see them.

3 remarked, "It is good we are able to reverse."

Bella looked puzzled. "Were we compulsing? We weren't here?"

"We were going to lithium site. How did you feel?" enquired 3.

Bella thought about it. "I wasn't aware of anything until + spoke."

"That is how it is. Feel nothing," explained +.

"But if we feel nothing, how did you know *therefore* wasn't all there?" asked Bella.

+ was silent for a while. "Knew *therefore* was not right. Maybe if there is discord in the compulse we become aware of the compulse."

"What would happen if we keep going when there is a problem?" Bella asked.

"I don't know," replied 3, "maybe separate and go to different places."

Bella shivered at the thought of losing her companions, though it seemed likely they would misplace *therefore* at some stage. She looked around and spotted + moving towards them with speed. Two dots were flat out with the remaining one trying to revive them. The approach of + made the dot more frantic in his attempts, his jumps getting higher and presumably harder. As a method of restoring anything, it appeared contrary, but it seemed to work with the dots as they slowly filled out into small spheres. As + stood next to them, one resumed the flattened position.

"When compulse you must concentrate," + was elongating over the dots and his tone was stern. "Next time we leave you."

Bella couldn't help smiling as the dots filled out and laboriously came together into their proper shape. 3 turned towards the dots.

"*Therefore,*" he shouted with authority, "Get ready. We are going to compulse."

"Again?" was the reply, reluctance in the tone.

"We compulse, therefore we go," 3 continued.

"Okay, okay." The dots moved to be beside 3. "Just tell us when to stop."

Bella watched them. But they were not beside 3 anymore. She wondered how much mischief they could get into. Then she saw them, one dot residing on each of 3's arms, for want of a better description. She sniffed the air, she could smell petrol and the smell wasn't stronger in any one direction but seemed to be all around them. This time they had compulsed. The petrol smell was the new site.

"This is lithium," 3 declared as he shook himself. All three dots fell off him, rolling away slowly but stopping at their proper shape, if at a slight angle.

"Why does it smell like petrol?" asked Bella.

"Lithium easily reacts with other substances and corrodes quickly so has to be stored under the cover of petroleum." 3 patiently offered the information.

"Lithium is also highly flammable," added +.

Bella reassured herself this was only an information site, it didn't physically contain these risks. But somewhere on the outside, there was actually this situation. Knowing about lithium was no doubt a clever discovery but then we undo all that intelligence by using it in ways that can cause more harm than good. While congratulating ourselves at how clever we are, we ignore the consequences of our action. And the consequences, those known or still to be found, should be as important as the discovery itself. Maybe we would then realize the discovery is not so important after all or that there are other ways to the same end. It would involve a lot of thinking about a lot of possibilities. Bella smiled. It's a lot of therefores. That could be why he kept getting into difficulties, he was experiencing consequential overload because it is his function is to work out all the possible reactions. We say we do that, but are usually just shocked when things go wrong. And then there are the consequences we ignore and carry on until our own creations can finally destroy everything.

She shrugged. A single fact, lithium, she will focus on that, without any preconceived ideas about what may or may not happen. That should be easy here since she had no idea about anything anyway.

"We'd best look around and find some sort of connection to Tony and Cassie."

"Certainly." 3 moved beside her with + slightly ahead of them and *therefore*, surprisingly all three of him, hovering nearby.

Again the images slowed whenever they were being looked upon. Drugs, in tablet form, were being endlessly poured into a triangle counter that never filled. Three dots became part of the cascade.

"Lithium salts are used as a mood stabilizer," explained 3, "though it may not work on *therefore*."

Bella moved on. A mound of grease glistened beside her.

"This was one of the first benefits discovered for lithium," said 3, pointing to the grease. "Because it is tolerant of heat, it was used in the lubricants for aircraft engines during the second world war."

Bella stopped. "Engines, that might be a connection. The site wouldn't just be older engines, would it?"

3 was prevented from answering by a loud slap. The grease had reared up and plunged down on *therefore*. It was smearing outwards and the dots were trying to extricate themselves from the slimy mess.

"What are these and who are you?" asked a voice. It had come from the grease, and with the dots still trying to pull out of the substance, the grease slid slowly towards Bella. "You are not lithium," it said.

Bella stood still. "We are searching for two children. They are here," she replied, accustomed now to holding conversations with bits of information.

"No," said grease.

3 waved his type to encompass more than he knew. "Not *here*. Here in space."

Grease rose up again, causing the three dots to fall out, sliding across the floor into 3. He rolled onto them to keep them still.

"In Corld?" asked Grease.

"What is Corld?" enquired 3.

Grease fell into a soft mound. "You do not know?" It quivered, giving off sparkles of light. "But you look for children." He twisted into a coil of shiny curves. It swung about and found the three dots, who immediately jumped to the top and in a sliding downward spiral, came to stop at Bella's feet. They continued this game as grease changed shape but continued to speak. "There is another space, other places where information goes. It distorts our meanings," Grease explained as he briefly loomed over Bella, one dot falling unnoticed in her hair. "We are compulsed to this place and put into information that is very twisted already." To emphasise the point, he became a tight coil, so tight the other two dots exploded out of him. "We come back here, sometimes not meaning the same as before. We fight to not be compulsed there again." He collapsed into a soft, shiny mound. Three dots immediately jumped on him. "That is Corld"

It was the same description that disturbed the mathematical symbols. Now they knew its name.

"How do you know you are being compulsed to...to Corld?" asked Bella.

Grease pulsed faintly. "It is different. The compulse is harder as if the space is thick. If concentrate, have time to recognize a Corld compulse and disrupt it."

"Are children in those places?" asked Bella, feeling the small dread in her heart grow a bit larger.

"Yes, they create the ideas and they use us to express them."

"And Corld, has it always been here?"

3 was beside Bella. "We do not know. But we are aware of it now and also aware of ourselves as bits of information because our meanings are being altered."

Why was information being collected only to be distorted? What was the distortion trying to describe? She wondered if Corld, or whatever was causing it, knew there was a consciousness growing amongst the information bits. Maybe that is want it wants. No, it can't be because the consciousness is against Corld. So it must be the distorted information it wants. And why the children? They do have uninhibited imaginations and intense patience when trying to master an aspect of the computer world. They become so focused. Is it possible for the information they are focusing on to become stronger because it is being understood and used? After all, that is how things remain vigorous. They have to be used, whether it is a house or boat, muscles or brain. Maybe Corld recognizes the children as sources of information and what if it found a way to gather that information?

She wondered what would happen if you were in Corld just wandering around, looking, not creating ideas. Probably be noticed, just like the third light to the cigarettes. Noticed by what though? What does Corld look like? Grease and 3 were still talking, + was investigating the site and *therefore*, as usual, she couldn't immediately spot. She felt they had to keep moving. She spoke, her voice loud with apprehension.

"We should select another image, 3."

A searing red colour infused around them. It was spectacular in its redness. Bella started to feel as if she was burning. Her skin was contracting at the heat. Suddenly, it stopped.

"The lithium flame," explained 3. "It burns red and is used in fireworks."

"Fireworks," gasped Bella. She called + and stood beside 3. "That is a link to Tony. He loved what they could do." It was a connection and she was relieved to find a site that is one of his latest interests. It was also good they would be moving again.

A protrusion from Grease slapped down three dots and slid them towards 3. + told them to pay attention to the compulse. "It is to fireworks. Do not be distracted." Each dot jumped onto one of 3's arms and waited.

Grease arched over Bella. "The children will be in Corld. We will watch here for information on your children or if you require help."

"Thank you Grease." She found the last very difficult to say, her mouth suddenly unable to form speech. There was a great heaviness in her body. She was lying down and she thought her eyes were open but she couldn't see anything. Weight seemed to be draining from her, pinning her down. She was feeling nauseous. She tried to keep from vomiting because she couldn't move her head, it was too heavy. She didn't know where she was or what was happening. She felt dreadful. Her body was collapsing, becoming a massive, heavy blob. She wondered if she was dying and then wondered why. Her head was aching now, a slow throb that could hardly be contained in her being. She wanted something to make it stop, even death, though that seemed inevitable now. Something else was happening. Her ankle was gripped in a vice. She wanted to cry out but could only silently plead with it not to move her, as she would be torn in two. The pressure remained, becoming tighter. Another wave of nausea surged over her. She waited for the end, either of her or the nausea, she didn't care which. The pressure on her ankle lessened. She took a breath and found she could swallow again. The horrible sensation of melting into the floor had stopped. She lay still, not wanting to do anything to start again any of those sensations. Drops were falling on her face. Maybe it was raining.

"It is good, a great relief." It was 3 speaking, anxiety in his voice despite the words. "*Therefore* was certain jumping up and down on you would revive you as it does them. Sadly, we could not know of anything else to do."

Even slowly, Bella found it was an effort to sit up. 3 and

therefore were beside her. She couldn't see +.

"Thank you...very much." She held her head. "But what happened?"

"Everything stopped," said 3.

Bella made herself think. She was in a computer. When everything stops it is because the computer has been turned off or the screen freezes. Surely this Corld would not turn itself off.

"How did you feel it?" She looked around. "And where is +?"

3 was silent for awhile. *Therefore* was now sitting on her shoulders and had discovered a new game. The dots were jumping high enough to entangle themselves in her hair and the competition seemed to be which dot could become so entangled it could not break free.

"We could sense being taken away, not like the compulse. It was quicker. We were going back to mathematical site. You were staying. We decided it better if we stay too so we compulse hard to not go. But you seemed to be disappearing. We know not where, we held onto you. + must not have been able to remain."

Now she couldn't think. They were not complete without +, not so strong. "He would be back with the other symbols at the mathematics site?" she asked hopefully.

"Yes," 3 replied, though Bella knew he could not be sure.

She smiled at him then remembered the vice like grip. "Keeping me here needed a very strong hold, 3. It must have been difficult for you."

"No. Not me, it was Grease."

Bella saw Grease now. He was stretching and compressing himself repeatedly. "I am nearly ready to show you my site. I needed to become rigid for the strength to keep you here."

Bella remembered they had been about to compulse to the fireworks site. She looked around. There were engines, explosions of light but colour seemed to be missing and the whole site seemed to be dulled by what could be haze.

"I am sorry Grease, but what is your site?"

"Lithium as a lubricant," he replied, still stretching. "Any sort of protection really," he added proudly.

"The stopping affected the compulse and we moved back here with Grease," said 3.

Bella looked at him. We are not at the fireworks site, she thought, and it had seemed like the best place to find Tony and Cassie, especially now in the disappointment of missing it. A new thought came to her. "Would the computer at home have stopped as well, breaking the connection to your site?"

"Do not know, Bella. The symbols will do their best...and + will give them more information."

"Yes," said Bella. There was not much else she could say. She had to find Tony and Cassie before she could even wonder at what they would do when they were together again.

"This site involves engines anyway," said Bella, "I am sure we can find another connection."

As she said it, she saw an endless line of connections. The amount of information in a computer was immense. Not all of it was accurate and it changed with interpretation as well. Tony and Cassie could be on any one of a billion connections. This may take a lot of time which she didn't think she had. Maybe this was not the right way to approach it. Grease said himself that Corld was filled with incorrect intent, so much so they had become aware of it and tried to avoid it. Where they are travelling now is not Corld. There is no evil intent here. They are just moving from one computer site to another when they should be trying to enter the sites through which Corld is operating. They will have to enter the places the bits of information have been trying to avoid, just like she avoids those sites on her computer that indulge in cruelty and abuse. They will be able to access Corld. She knows it. Wickedness exists all around everyone, it is just invisible to those who are not part of it. If you want to see it or try its pitiless offerings, that world will find you. Sometimes though, you can find it yourself. She did once, before Justin, before Tony and Cassie. A friendship, that finest of things, she had left it, ignored and unhappy while she chased that which others said she should and which would be better for her. It was not, or not enough to scour away the guilt and distress at hurting a loved one so much. Why hadn't she been able to say no to these others? It would have been easier to say no way back then than to continually feel the sadness and silently utter the many apologies forever after. How young she had been. No, that is not right. That is not an excuse as she can sometimes feel influenced again by those that want to redefine the things and ideas she cares about, making them less, making her scared so she will behave more for her own interests, with less compassion for other beings…heedless of consequences. But she knows to keep looking into her heart to remind herself who and what she cares about and to not be disloyal to that love or to herself. The trick is to remain confident that the heart does know best and that she has the strength to not betray what it knows.

She explained to 3, *therefore* and Grease that she also knows what it is like to lose your own meaning, to act unkindly through fear and selfishness. "Maybe," she suggested, "it is not only intelligence Corld perceives but vulnerability which makes for easier entrapment."

They were silent, Grease eventually falling still, satisfied with his consistency.

"I am ready to go to Corld," he said.

"It is where we have to go," said 3.

Therefore became his proper shape on top of 3. "We go, therefore we know even if we don't," he declared.

Bella smiled with gratitude as they moved closer together. What an odd bunch we are, thought Bella, but she felt strong because in Corld, they will discover even more of their capabilities.

"It will be somewhere we feel exposed and wrong and we will figure out Corld," 3 declared.

Tony and Douglas

The images grew and it seemed as if the space would not be able to contain them. Tony was ecstatic. The capacity of his engine to hold, gas, fluid and even metal became obvious. Now he could experiment with more effective quantities to make sound slow down or scatter. He would have to keep track of the mathematical equations and ratios for each experiment with the fuel or substances. Accurately recording these results will take up quite a bit of time. Maybe Cassie would like to help him out with the ongoing maths and results.

"Cassie, look at this." Tony didn't take his eyes off the screen. Douglas, who had been immersed in the dimensions of the engine, now looked at all the images. They were more complex than what they had been working on. He turned from the images to look around. There was no Cassie. He shouted for her and got up from his seat to be able to search more of the space. His realization at what had happened came out as a groan.

"The little idiot. Why wasn't she paying attention?"

"Who wasn't paying attention?" asked Tony.

"Cassie. She didn't come here with us."

Puzzled, Tony looked at him. "What do you mean here? Of course she is here. She came with me."

"No Tony. We have moved."

"Moved?" exclaimed Tony looking around, "moved where?"

"To somewhere else." Douglas quickly continued as he saw Tony was about to interrupt. "We are in a world structured like a computer, with many sites for information and ideas. The world is probably only limited by our need to know. When ideas grow towards other meanings, you can follow the ideas to relevant sites. We have done that, we have moved from the fireworks site that trapped you and Cassie." Douglas wondered about that word, 'trapped.' He had never thought of it like that before. Tony wasn't interrupting now but listening with eyes large. "Anyway," Douglas resumed, "the sites are great for ideas as you can follow any line of experimentation, no matter how complex. If an equation or an idea is wrong, your work will not implode but still follow the sequences through so you can see where it is wrong and what will happen as it goes wrong. Our idea grew to involve more than the fireworks site." He sighed again. "Unfortunately, Cassie must have been distracted as this happened and she didn't come with us."

Tony waited for more but Douglas didn't know what else to add. Tony looked back at the images.

"You mean," he began, "we can keep going with our ideas to an end result even if it is impossible in practice?"

"Yes."

"We could create an engine for all the sound distortions I can imagine through tests with the images?"

Douglas also looked at the images. Their engine wasn't to scale. To be able to see the compartments, they had increased its size. He could see that another problem to making it work was to ensure the outer shell had enough strength to withstand the different levels of violence going on and still have a light weight. The metal they were using now would tear apart because it was too small to give it the necessary strength. So what to change: the metal, the nature of the explosions or the fuels? That was his work and his ideas and equations were with his images on the fireworks site. He didn't think it would be a problem transferring them to here, especially as it would benefit Tony's work. A slight unease came over him as he wondered again about who wanted the benefit from Tony's work and why? Are the images totally under their own control?

The excitement diffused from Tony as he quietly looked at his engine. "Cassie would be impressed with this if she were here." He turned to Douglas. "We had better look for her, I suppose." Turning away from his images, he peered into the darkness. "Where could she go?"

Douglas was thoughtful. "She should be at the fireworks site because she cannot move around without images. But that is probably a good reason to move around."

Tony looked back at Douglas, wondering why he sounded worried. This place is for ideas, how could anything hurt Cassie? "Why does she have to move around?"

"I think she would be safer if she did. Not having your own images means you do not belong here."

"Who would know or even care about that?"

Douglas was silent in an effort to make coherent his own thoughts. "The images are why anybody is here. The ideas are important." He came to a stop. "Without images, Cassie is useless and I suspect this world notices what is unproductive."

"Uh huh," said Tony, unsure about how ideas were somehow threatening Cassie. He knew his sister however. "I can't imagine Cassie waiting for me to go back and get her. Not that I would know how to do that." He stared at his images. "So what could Cassie do to move on?"

"Actually, she was trying to look for a way home," said Douglas.

"She wanted to go home?" Tony sounded incredulous. "How was she doing that?"

"Checking out the images of others at the site, looking for knowledge that would connect to other sites, eventually leading to home."

"So all you have to do is find a connection to our home and you would be transported there?" Tony asked.

Douglas was smiling now. "Yes, I think that is how it could happen. There is probably a bit more to it than that but we can work it out as we go along."

"It should be easy," said Tony, with a touch of mockery.

"The connections won't be obvious so we have to know our own subject as well as every other subject to identify the correct trail."

Douglas gave Tony a friendly punch on the arm. "And be quick witted to stay ahead, don't forget that. That is how you move around this world."

They both faced the images again. The engine was revolving, showing all its components while periodically showering firework lights at different angles. The explosions seemed to occur randomly.

"Did you hear that?" exclaimed Tony. "I am sure that came from the fish firework. If it did, we may have created a delay in the noise." He stopped, suppressing his excitement. "Cassie wouldn't care about that though and wouldn't even look at it."

"Maybe we should start from somewhere else," said Douglas. "Cassie was talking to the other kids on the fireworks site."

Tony, surprise all over his face, was looking at Douglas. "Was she? Now I think, she did mention others. Trust Cassie to find people to talk to."

Douglas nodded. "One of them was a younger kid. If we could get amongst his images, we may be able to contact her or he could pass a message to her."

Tony remembered his own focus on the images to the exclusion of everything else, including Cassie and she was his sister. "Would he do that, pass a message on?"

Douglas shrugged. "Who knows? There may be a spark of life left in some of these kids."

"It's a start anyway," agreed Tony. "What's his name?"

Douglas had to think. He didn't know, never wanted to ask either. The other kids on the sites he has visited never interested him. He only took notice of Cassie because she had no images of her own. It was unusual and he thought he might learn more about this world by watching what it did to her. He was expecting her to suddenly disappear, probably in a spectacular way, but she hadn't. He tried to listen in on her conversations to find out what she knew. But she really did know nothing. What was that kid's name? He didn't think names were important here, though Cassie insisted on telling everyone her name. It is the kids' knowledge that is important. They themselves don't really matter. But the kid had made a point of his name.

"Mick or Michael, that's it." He looked at Tony. "He was involved in the trajectory of fireworks. All we have to do is figure out an interesting facet of this and it may be passed onto his images."

Tony looked skeptical. "What, and then tack on, 'and by the way, tell Cassie we are looking for her?'"

Douglas smiled at him. "Got it in one, though not those exact words. More of a code Cassie will recognize."

Tony thought. "We never had codes at home. She can stay quiet when she wants to and doesn't mind who hears her when she has an opinion." Douglas waited and soon Tony continued. "Dates though. All Mum's pin numbers are our birthdays."

"That would work," said Douglas. "Numbers or equations are easy to add to information."

"Is it really necessary to hide what we are doing?" asked Tony.
"Yes."

"You were serious earlier when you said this world uses us in some way?"

"Yes." Douglas faced Tony but he didn't know what else to say that could reassure him.

Tony swallowed then smiled turning to the images. "Because we don't know what the bad guys look like here, no one must know what we are doing."

"Except for Cassie," countered Douglas, "and our advantage is that Cassie should pick up any connection to you faster than this world will. But we had better keep going with our ideas on this engine. We should continue to do what is normal for here."

"We need your images from the firework site," said Tony.

"Some of them are here. It must be okay to combine ideas."

They worked the images, more of Douglas' arriving all the time. Tony calculated the ratio of substances to slow down sound while Douglas tried to fit these quantities in appropriate metal spaces. They didn't work silently. They argued points, discussed problems and any exclamation of success was tempered by the calculations of the other.

"But Douglas," Tony was defending his latest configurations, "the firework is going one way and the sound will travel at right angles to the flight so there will be less forward force on that metal there." With his finger he bulged the area of the image relating to his point.

Douglas sighed at the complications they were creating. "But you will lose momentum because of the angle of sound which will be smaller and will direct more force onto that metal than you have calculated. More importantly though, this is something that may go to Mick as it involves trajectory of an object."

Tony smiled at Douglas. "Yes. What we need to know is the angle of deviation caused by the opposing direction of sound and where is Cassie." He turned back to the images. "It would be interesting to know. Your smaller dimensions may be okay to use, but we won't find out if we have to work my birth date into the angles we are considering. Mick will think we are idiots."

"That is why he will notice and could answer just to tell us how wrong we are. What are your dates?"

"Seventeen, eight, ninety five."

"Yeah, see what you mean. I wonder if being stupid is a way of being sent home. But here goes." Douglas struggled to keep the images in the new equation. It seemed that there were some mistakes the images wouldn't be part of. He had to work them, there was no anticipation of what was required because the birth date in the equation made it illogical. It was hard work. "Right," he said finally, "let's hope that finds its way to Mick."

They continued to work on the engine, always mindful of information that could be used to convey messages to Cassie.

Douglas ordered hamburgers and fries. When the food arrived it looked delicious and Tony ate ravenously though he didn't think he was hungry.

"Douglas, surely you can get an explosion even with that amount of solids in the fuel. The sound effect would be great. It would be late and in a totally different direction. Maybe it wouldn't even be connected with the explosion." Tony's images were moving rapidly with his enthusiasm.

"If the sound is not related somehow, what is the point," Douglas responded.

Tony was briefly downcast which was reflected in his images as they also slowed down.

"It would be confusing," he finally answered. "And you could make a show of it somehow. Just have to put it together properly. Music does that all the time. Some music, the rhythms are incomprehensible." He faltered a bit. "I don't know. It could be something dramatic."

Douglas was also thinking. "You are right. It could be dramatically confusing. If you see an explosion you expect a noise or some destruction. If there was silent destruction and a massive noise in a totally different direction, what would you think happened?"

"Awesome. But because it is fireworks, it will be continuous. The confusion has to be choreographed."

"A good plan," agreed Douglas. He was quiet for a while. "But what connects it to your home?"

Tony shrugged. "The possibility it could be in any direction."

"Okay, let's take it from there," said Douglas who knew more about how impossible ideas can be formulated in this world. "Actually it will be easy as your calculations will destroy your engine, sending it not only in any direction, but in all."

Tony rolled his eyes. "If your metals could hold it, there would be no problem."

"The metals are wrong. I agree. What we should be doing is making container walls that will aid the sound. We need to experiment with metals that resonate, thereby helping with the volume and direction of the noise with less explosive force."

Tony was already experimenting with the vibrations of Douglas' metals. "Make sure the noise is correct. We want thunder, not the fall of a pebble."

"What about an echoing guitar riff along with the explosion," suggested Douglas, his fingers busy manipulating ores, "followed by the plaintive sound of the bagpipes lessening as the colours fade."

Tony giggled. "No, the mind shattering shrieks of instruments as the orchestra warms up."

Douglas was also laughing. "Everyone would run away. There would be no one to see the…, look at that," he exclaimed.

"What?' Tony was trying to control his images while looking at Douglas' side of the space.

"I think it was a message from Mick. Let me clear some of these images. You look as well. I don't think personal messages are encouraged so if it appears again it may be brief."

Tony was having trouble with his images. They seemed to be out of control. He used his fingers to pull them back but they wouldn't stay there. He kept his thoughts on the patterns he wanted the fireworks to follow but the images found more erratic trajectories. A few fell off the space. Then suddenly he saw the pattern the images were following: multiple trajectories and it was in the timing. One directional force enabled another easier passage, as did that one and so it went on. It was beautiful.

"Can you see it?" shouted Douglas.

Cassie, Tony belatedly remembered. He tore his eyes away from his images and tried to recognize something that could be a message. He saw a word, 'nuisance' and a few others but they never appeared together or along the same horizontal. It was frustrating trying to look everywhere at once, catching words that didn't make sense. Soon there were no more to be seen. The images had smothered them all.

"What words did you see?" asked Tony.

"'Sister', which would confirm it was about Cassie and from Mick." Douglas thought for a bit. "I think I saw 'looking' and 'fiend,' unless it was supposed to be 'friend'. 'Calculation' appeared, 'absurd' and 'not here'."

"'Nuisance' and 'calculation' are the only ones I can remember seeing," said Tony.

"'Nuisance' seems to further confirm Cassie is there with Mick. 'Fiend' or 'friend'? It has to be 'friend', though I can't imagine any kid here giving anything other than his images the amount of attention that could be called friendship." Douglas looked at Tony. "What do you make of it?"

"He must have received our calculation and knew it was absurd and either the answer to it is 'not here' or it is Cassie he is talking about." The message had not worked very well but they knew now it could be done.

Tony was staring at his images. The engine was still rotating, showing off the compartments and every now and then, one would explode, sending the coloured lights spinning in another direction. But floating across the engine were musical notes, pulsating with their own noise. The waves of vibration they created clashed with the momentum of the engine, stalling it, changing its direction and causing the fuel to burn and explode with erratic timing. It was in danger of destroying itself but the musical connotations continued to burn steadily.

"Have we moved again?" asked Tony, looking around.

"Music," exclaimed Douglas, "how did that happen?"

"We were talking about sound effects...." Tony nudged Douglas. "Look at the other guys here. They look half asleep and I can't hear anything. How does music come into this?"

Douglas looked and listened. Tony was right. The boys here were not focused on their images. They were looking around the space though not showing any interest in the arrival of Tony and Douglas, but that didn't mean anything anyway. It was weird that some of the boys were walking about. Douglas couldn't remember any boy wanting to leave his images. Now he could hear some music. It was muted but once aware of it, it seemed to become louder and come from everywhere.

"There is music here," he said. Douglas wondered if there had been a mistake. But he didn't think this world allowed mistakes. Maybe their attempts to use the images to find Cassie had been noticed. Why here though? The musical notes seemed to be integrating with their own ideas. Douglas had a sense they were tangling up the engine. Suddenly a mouth appeared in the top corner of the space. It was warty, moist and rubbery. Printing out of it were words.

You seem to be looking for someone.
There is no help here.

The mouth twisted into a sneering grin and slowly disappeared.

Douglas looked at Tony but he was staring at the boys. "They look more than half asleep, they look drugged," he said, pointing at a boy walking closer to them. "What is wrong with them?"

The boy stopped beside their space and stared back at them.

"Hi," said Tony. There was no reply. Tony turned to Douglas. "Are they zombies do you think?"

"Where did you guys come from?" The question came from the boy and to Tony's and Douglas' surprise, he didn't sound like a zombie at all. "Uh, hang on," he continued as he fiddled with his ears. After much probing, he drew out a congealed substance and smiled at them. "You will need something to plug your ears if you want to survive this place." He continued to smile at them but it slowly disappeared as Tony and Douglas remained silent in shock.

Finally they recovered. "Hey. I'm Douglas and this is Tony. What is this place?"

The boy relaxed with relief. "I was beginning to think I was too late and you were under the influence of this place already. It's music here but not the sort you want to listen to."

"Music?" queried Tony. "I don't hear anything."

"Don't pay it any notice," the boy shouted. "Damn, I have to put these things in again now." He returned the plugs to his ears.

"You're right," said Tony, "I can hear the music now. It's awful."

"I'm Ned," the boy explained in the loud voice of the deaf.

"The music is mind numbing and it takes over, you can't ignore it. Soon it is the only thing in your mind." He stopped and smiled at them, then seemed to remember conversation was impossible if he couldn't hear so he removed a plug from one ear. "You will need something to put in your ears. It helps to keep the music away," he finished.

"Where did you get your ear plugs from?" asked Tony.

Ned looked embarrassed "You don't really want to know."

Tony and Douglas waited expectantly for the explanation.

In a hesitant mumble, Ned admitted he always had trouble with belly button lint.

Tony looked doubtful about the necessity for such extremes.

"Believe me," says Ned, "you will need plugs of some sort."

He watched as Douglas searched in his pockets, but found nothing. "The trouble with this world is that nothing is generated, not even fluff or dirt in pockets. My navel has never been cleaner."

Douglas turned to Tony. "You are a recent arrival. Check your pockets for scrapings of anything." But Tony was not listening, instead, his face was turned upwards as if in rapture. "Tony!" they both yelled. Finally Tony turned to look at Douglas and Ned standing in front of him.

"How can this music that is nothing be so dangerous?"

Ned was concentrating on Tony, trying not to listen to the music.

"Because that is all there is here. You cannot change it and because it makes you so stupid you can't work on it anyway. Listen to it...no don't. It is nothing music, but it creeps into your mind and it doesn't leave."

"What is it doing here?" asked Douglas, "I mean, why would anybody want to write this stuff?"

"I also couldn't understand it," said Ned. "Then I thought, everyone interprets music differently and some write it down their way. Maybe this is music gone wrong somehow in the process. It reminds me of something further along, though not much, from that music we are forced to listen to, supposedly, to make waiting a better experience. Somebody must write it, a bit of Jimi Hendrix with a Bob Marley sound to make people think of beaches and fun and then slow it right down and take out the surprises so that it is unrecognisable anyway. It is nothing music."

"But at the sites before this one, what was the original purpose for creating the music?"

"Maybe it was experimenting with a way to tame people?" suggested Ned. Douglas looked at Ned: someone else has recognized a threat in this place.

"Why can't we turn it down?" asked Tony.

Douglas looked around. Finally he turned back to Tony and Ned who were busy fashioning ear plugs out of bits of paper, cotton strands and general fluff from Tony's pockets. "It feels like a room," Douglas was speaking aloud his thoughts, "they all do, but they aren't. There are not any walls." He sighed. "And Cassie wanted doors you could exit through. There are no switches, nothing to control our environment. But there is no environment to control." He stopped and pointed to the images. "That is all there is here and we are their dupes."

"Isn't that what you have always said?" asked Tony.

"Yes," said Douglas, "but I have to keep remembering because these," he waved his arm amongst the images, "make me forget."

Musical symbols scattered around Douglas' arm and Tony was alarmed to see them move down to settle over his engine, submerging it.

"Hey," he shouted, "be careful. And anyway, even if what you keep repeating is true, we still have to work through the images." He began salvaging his engine. "I hope the musical stuff hasn't infected or broken anything," he muttered.

Ned sat beside Tony. "What does it do?" he asked. The engine was struggling. It twisted and writhed against the embrace of the musical bars. A small explosion sounded and the engine broke a couple of the lines. It was squealing and Ned couldn't help but stare at it. "Is it injured?"

"No." Tony kept prompting the explosions and sounds, trying to help the engine twist through the entanglement of musical debris. "It is a sound distorter so it should be able to maneuver its way through this junk."

The notes surrounding the engine changed, some shriveled but others became bolder. The noises from the engine were endless and it was difficult not to cringe in sympathy with what sounded like cries of pain. Suddenly it was still. The musical symbols clambered all over it. Tony was frantic, busy strengthening his engine. Feeling helpless just watching, Ned joined in, trying to remove or shift the invading symbols. There was a loud explosion and Ned fell backwards off the seat as he was hit with a thick wave of air. He struggled to his feet, hoping the destruction was minimal. Tony was still sitting, gently turning his engine, looking for damage. "It seems to be okay," he declared.

"We had better keep it strong," said Ned, sitting back down beside Tony, "because those musical symbols are still here." He eyed them with suspicion, readying himself for another fight.

Tony took his eyes away from his engine to glare at the musical symbols and wondered if he was imagining their regrouping maneuvers.

"What have you two done?" Douglas was beside them, shouting, "and put your earplugs in."

Tony's first reaction was to listen. Douglas thumped him. "Your earplugs," he repeated.

The music was louder, clawing into their minds and leaving them helpless.

Tony and Ned returned to inspecting the engine, Douglas peered around. Finally, they felt confident enough to each remove one plug.

"This place does feel like the end," said Douglas in a whisper. "There are no ideas here, just the stupor of surrender."

"I have wondered about that," said Ned. "Hester kept saying it was an amazing world of ideas, but I can't see any of that."

Tony and Douglas were looking at him. "Hester is my sister."

Tony groaned. "You have one of those too."

"You see," continued Ned, "she found this world on her

computer. I don't think it was this site, otherwise she would not have thought it such a grand thing. But places where she could compose her music and she could hear it played. She said what was in her head seemed to be generating a response on the computer. As if her instruments had gained life and were playing her ideas." Ned stopped. "I used to laugh at her, thinking she put all sorts of weird imaginings onto computers when all she had done was discover something else it could do." Ned looked down at his shuffling feet. Tony was nodding in sympathy.

"Yeah, they don't think properly," he said.

Douglas started to say something but decided against it. After all, he didn't have a sister.

"I went into her room for something and she was peering at her screen." Ned gazed into the distance. Douglas watched anxiously for signs of succumbing to the music but Ned was only remembering. "I mean, she was really concentrating, she hadn't heard me come in shouting my questions. She was mumbling something about monsters I think. I stood beside her to see what she was looking at and the next thing I know, I am here, with this awful music and these dead people." Ned waved his arm over the site. "And no monsters or whatever it was she was looking at. I wish they were here. It would be a bit of excitement at least."

"Monsters?" asked Douglas. "What do monsters have to do with this place?"

"I don't know," said Ned, "but if you want to know anything, ask that fellow over there." Ned pointed into the darkness. "Ben his name is and he looks the deadest of the lot. But he is clever, maybe even cleverer than Corld. It is from him I have learnt about this place. He does talk but only when he wants to."

"Who is Corld?" asked Tony.

"It is this place," said Ned. "Not just here, but all those sites that have some sort of awareness are part of Corld. It is a computer world with an agenda. Ben explained that to me."

"If he is so clever," asked Douglas, "why is he here?"

"Ask him yourself. I couldn't understand when he explained

it to me."

"I will talk to him. See if he knows how to control the movement through the sites."

"Don't know if we will be able to go anywhere," said Tony with sadness, "my engine is looking pretty sick."

"It will be alright," remarked Ned with a confidence that surprised Tony and Douglas. "There are a few things at work here, other things that can help, according to Ben. Didn't fully understand all he said, but he sees the weaknesses of Corld." Ned looked at them grinning. "The problem is coordinating the connections between here and the outside because the outside has to be in a receptive state. I just worry when we see the connections towards home, Hester will be on the toilet or something."

"You two keep working on the engine and any other image," said Douglas, "I will find Ben." He looked around. "The deadest one you say," he murmured as he walked away.

Tony and Ned started on the images. The musical symbols were all over the engine again.

"They keep coming," exclaimed Tony in despair. "How do we keep them off?"

"Maybe we should concentrate on how the music can benefit the engine," suggested Ned. "These symbols, if they are strong enough to cause damage, maybe we can use them as another type of material to reinforce the engine."

Tony sat up straighter, his mind picturing where and how it could be strengthened. If these incredibly persistent notes are matter, they could act as a spontaneous repair kit. He turned to Ned, deflating suddenly. "Would that mean we have to listen to it?"

But Ned had caught Tony's initial enthusiasm and was working the musical symbols. "Yes, but we would be listening to it as something we can use, not music necessarily. It may make a difference."

Tony placed the ear plug on the seat between him and Ned. "As long as they are close by, we can block out the music whenever we feel it is taking control."

"Right, and we keep an eye on each other," said Ned. "Let's start then."

Tony surreptitiously pushed Ned's well used plug further away from his own and then they were both busy with the images.

Eventually Ned asked, "How are we going to do this?"

Tony sat back. "I don't know." He thought for a bit, watching Ned remove the symbols. It was difficult, like removing ants from a jar of honey. The engine was breaking away with the symbols and though they may be strengthening the engine, they were suffocating it as well.

"Maybe we can use this stubbornness to shore up the walls of the engine as well as give strength to the explosions." Tony became more excited as he talked. The possibility of using the character of this music was much the same as using explosions to control sound and direction. He tried to explain this idea to Ned. The engine will move to the beat of the music ("Does it have one?" asked Ned), thereby giving strength to the engine's structure because the music is resisting change, even change through the power of explosions.

The engine was trying to move to the beat and its contortions were amazing to watch as it tried to find a rhythm.

"It is certainly flexible," remarked Ned. But controlling the direction of the music was difficult. The notes managed to out-maneuver their efforts, taking the control of the engine away from the boys.

Discouragement lessened the concentration of Tony. "Ned, how were you trying to connect with your sister?"

Ned was quiet with remembering, then he started. "It was more hoping Hester could connect with me. Landing here was horrible, I didn't know what had happened. Then there were these boys, just walking around, not interested in anything. And the music, I couldn't think, it was always in my ears. I fashioned my earplugs and was able to take note of what was around me. The images seemed to be the only other thing here and I could only hope, seeing I got here through concentrating on the image at Hester's computer, I could go back the same way." Ned stopped. "It sounds vague, but I really didn't know what this place was or what was happening. I tried to reproduce something like Hester's work but the images kept reverting to how they were or became gibberish." He indicated Tony's engine and the efforts to keep it how it should be. "Nothing worked. I even thought of taking out my earplugs and listening to the music. Maybe it could explain this place. But the more I saw of the boys here, the more I believed the music was dead in this site. To listen was somehow dangerous." He grinned at Tony. "Thankfully I like my music loud and controversial. I have always been suspicious of music that doesn't make you feel like doing something great."

Tony could only nod. He didn't want to interrupt and his engine still needed help.

"Anyway," continued Ned, "I went to every boy here and asked how to make the images work. Even if it was just an on switch I had missed. It was creepy because none of them reacted. But I persisted because I hadn't thought of anything else. Got the fright of my life when one of them did react. That was Ben and he said I should have only one idea." Ned shook his head. "One idea, how impossible is that. Out of all Hester's ideas, I had to choose one to save my life. But I tried on neglected symbols floating by and it was interesting what the images threw up at me. Nothing relevant to Hester, but I started to understand how to work them and see what was in this world because the images caused other things to happen. Once I thought I saw one of those monsters Hester had been mumbling about and there have been messages from other places."

Tony was smiling. "Monsters, I wonder what they do here? I know messages are sent but it is difficult to recognize them as they appear quickly and are not that obvious."

Ned was shaking his head. "One of the messages said quite clearly, *'Bella is looking, therefore is in trouble.'* Whoever she is, she must also be trying to find a way out."

He realized Tony was staring at him, muttering.

"Are you okay?" asked Ned anxiously, reaching for the

earplugs.

Tony seemed to come out of his daze. "A coincidence no doubt, but my mother's name is Bella."

"Oh...." Ned didn't know what else to say. Here, in this place, in Corld, it seemed silly to say something was impossible.

Because he was returning to them, walking towards the back of the images, Douglas could see Tony and Ned and they both looked worried. He wondered if he could see them because the images and Tony's engine were not actually there anymore. He hurried his steps.

"Something has happened," Ben said behind him.

Douglas had nearly forgotten him in his initial panic over the images, but now felt calmer. Whatever had happened, Ben would be able to help. Maybe though, he had spent too long talking to Ben, too long away from Tony, but what Ben knew of Corld had absorbed his attention.

Ben came to Corld willingly and he didn't need images to do so. He comes to rest his mind, he had said. A mind that moves around, that can see the problems and contradictions people create in societies and how impossible the solutions are when the problems are not acknowledged. But he tries, day by day, to live in this confusion his mind forces on his awareness. Sometimes, there is too much stupidity and cruelty and he has to retreat, just to rest, to get away from the inconsistent reasoning for shameless destruction. Douglas was skeptical and gave a little snort. Ben smiled at him and closed his eyes once more.

Trying to regain Ben's attention, Douglas voiced his doubts. "But this place is for ideas, how can the mind relax here with so much to discover and learn?"

Without opening his eyes Ben answered gently. "Ideas, plural, yes. But only Corld sees all of them. Everyone else has only one idea in their heads. It is what Corld wants. A single idea is easier to control."

Douglas sat down beside Ben. He thought about his own ideas and images. Reinventing gunpowder, he had told Cassie. Taking ideas from others and sending out his own. But he hadn't been. He didn't ask for the ideas of others. They had just arrived amongst his own images. There was no sharing if that meant talking things out with others. He was receiving only what someone else thought he needed to move along. To move along to what though? Something Corld wanted. Douglas shook his head and grinned. He thought he had been so clever.

Still without opening his eyes, Ben said, "The boys...and girls, there are a few here, but generally the girls do not become so obsessed with one idea and the wonder of their own cleverness, so are not seduced so easily. The boys," he repeated, "have their one idea and Corld encourages it, which makes them feel important. They focus more and the idea becomes everything. They rely on it for their self esteem and reason for being. The consequences of their ideas ceased to matter long before this, probably the boys never thought about it and Corld certainly wouldn't want any sense of right and wrong developing."

"So we are on the right track now," suggested Douglas hopefully, "the images can lead you out of here." He stopped. "There is a way out of Corld, isn't there?"

Ben was quiet for a while, then sighed deeply. He sat up straighter, opened his eyes and stared at Douglas. "Yes, there is an exit, though the boys by then may only exist as the container for the idea. And the trail of the child's journey through Corld is marked by the progression of the images."

"A complicated trail though," Douglas replied, remembering the surprise of this music site.

"No," said Ben, "it is not complicated. Corld couldn't work otherwise. The trail is obvious because it follows the inevitable line of one obsessive idea."

"But Tony and I arrived here and we were working on fireworks."

"You have, against many odds, found the weakness in Corld. The control is less effective if there is a mingling of ideas as that initiates the concept of options. That is what you did."

"No, Tony and I were working on the same thing."

Ben just looked at him. Tony wondered if Ben knew as much

as he made out. Then he remembered the message to Michael. There had been a third mind amongst their images and also Cassie had been with Michael and her mind could have been on anything. There would have been many influences pulling on the images.

Douglas looked at Ben. "I still don't understand. How did you get here?"

"Think of nothing," said Ben. He smiled at Douglas' doubtful expression. "And make the thought of nothing so impenetrable, it becomes a channel. Such a strong channel it should contain an idea. Corld is now fooled and opens this world to you. Enter if you dare," Ben leant closer to Douglas, his smile gone, "because Corld is powerful and dangerous. You found his weakness but Corld still managed to send you to this." Ben waved his arm. "A dead site where you end up when the usefulness of the idea has ended." He relaxed again but Douglas was not offering any conversation. "So," continued Ben, "what is it you want me to do?"

Corld had opened up for Douglas through Ben's eyes, far more than he had ever let himself discover. Feeling as if he had only just arrived, Douglas could only mutter a request for help. Ben stood and with a wave of his arm, invited Douglas to return to Tony and Ned. He knew Ben was following but wondered what those two had been up to.

Nothing much seemed to have been gained, Douglas noticed. The musical symbols were still trying to envelop Tony's engine. They were both still working hard but all that effort was only enough to keep the engine from being swamped—for now.

"This music is determined to stay at nothing music," said Tony. "Can't change its beat, can't turn it off and it gets in everywhere. What a horrible site this one is."

"Well, it is an end site," said Ben.

"'End'?" asked Tony. "Does that mean we are close to getting out of here?"

"No, it is the end of the boys and their ideas. There are no idea trails that leave here, because there are no minds here."

They all looked at Ben. He shrugged and continued. "We need to reenter Corld where there are trails that go somewhere. To do that, we have to make the music do something, at least give it a beat that is not so stuck in apathy."

"That is what we have been trying to do," Tony groaned, "but we can't capture all the notes."

Ned nodded in agreement. "They are fighting us, and winning, I think."

Douglas was grinning. "Apathy, in contradiction to its meaning, is a very strong force."

"Oh yes," said Ben, "and the consequences of apathy perpetuate that strength to be even more of nothing. Doing and being nothing becomes a formidable opponent. So let us see if we can make the notes pay attention." He examined the engine. "A clever sound distorter." Tony smiled and it became bigger when, under Ben's fingers, his machine seemed to be bolder and the notes had to work harder to collect round it. But they were still managing to coalesce in the engine's structure.

"All the notes need to go through I think," said Tony, "because any left behind could ruin it totally."

Ned spoke up, if a bit hesitantly as he now knew what they were up against. "That will require more strength than we have. These notes seem to have the power of Corld behind them."

"What about your channel?" asked Douglas of Ben.

Tony looked at Ben in surprise. "Do you have images here?"

"No, it is his mind," answered Douglas.

Ben looked at Douglas for a long time. "The music will have to become an idea and Ned has already figured out the power of the music is Corld." Ned opened his mouth to say something, but again he couldn't think of anything that would be effective against the intensity of the music. Ben was continuing but now looking at the engine. "If I can collect some of the notes in my mind and funnel them into your engine, its function as a sound distorter should produce some sort of beat. You will have to help it though, to produce even a tiny rhythm from these dead notes.

But that may be all we need."

Ned looked at the other boys walking around, oblivious to everything. "If you did, would this place disappear?"

"No, unfortunately," replied Ben. "I would be only controlling it for a few seconds to go through the machine. The music will have continued to perpetuate itself." He thought for a bit more. "Doing this means I will have to listen to it."

This made Tony, Douglas and Ned more nervous than anything he had said previously. Tony and Ned spoke at once, voting against this option and even Douglas asked if it could be done any other way.

Ben smiled. "You have reminded me how awful the music is. I will be mindful of it." He was quiet with concentration and Tony, Douglas and Ned fell silent, watching him carefully. Ben sat and became very still. The others put back both their ear plugs so they could concentrate on Ben's face only, though they didn't know the difference between a look of great thought or one of mindless thought. Nothing seemed to be happening and even Ben's breathing slowed down. He remained silent, his eyes fixed on the engine. They sat around him, now and then glancing at each other to see if someone had any suggestions. Tony started a whispered monologue on how his sound distorter should be working. Suddenly it bucked and sounds emerged as if it was under extreme pressure. They could hear it even through their earplugs

"It's like something at the end of a Roger Waters composition," Douglas observed

"It will need a miracle to survive this," commented Ned.

Ben's voice startled them, especially as it seemed to come from so far away. "Help the sound distorter move the music."

They all jumped, remembering this was their role in this procedure but were helpless to think of what to do as they watched it expand and contort.

"It looks like it should vomit," remarked Ned.

Tony fiddled with his engine and a noise did escape though it sounded more like breaking wind.

Ned sniffed the air. "It smells like something has died."

Ben moved beside them, stretching his muscles as if after a relaxing nap. "Look around boys. We have moved to somewhere else," he said.

Cassie

Cassie was alone. The images had been swallowed by the blackness and now it surrounded her. Her initial fright was disappearing enough for Cassie to hope she was alone and the creature was not close by, watching.

"They finally left you." She flinched, but now had something on which to focus. She turned, her eyelight catching the creature. His shape changed continuously. A protuberance would reach out for her then suddenly withdraw as if she were the grotesque one. A dark hole appeared and puffy lips grew around it. Other lips travelled around its body and settled below the first mouth. She couldn't see any eyes, then suddenly they were there. Two ogling eyeballs, seaming with dark colours and one was hanging down as if it had been pulled out. She is sure it is the same creature that escaped from Tony's images. It has the same malignant, knowing look. If it is in some way connected to us, thought Cassie, maybe he could be a link, though she didn't know how she would use him. She told herself to think of him like that rather than a ghastly apparition belonging to this world. She stood straight and looked down into its dripping eyes. Though asserting herself like this was not very effective when the creature's eyes kept moving and changing.

"You distracted me," she told him boldly.

His eyes were definitely looking elsewhere and she didn't want to wait for his attention to return to her. She suspected the creature would always be somewhere close.

Michael, she would find Michael. Her eyelight pierced the

blackness, searching. A faint warm greasy something slipped across her leg.

"They are not here."

Cassie wanted to move away but when she looked down, the creature's loose eye was curved around her leg and it was looking up at her face. She took a deep breath and moved her eyelight upwards.

"There he is." She had caught someone in her eyelight, thank goodness, though she wasn't sure if it was Michael, but any of them would do now. Slowly she brought her foot up. He was horrible, but she didn't want to rip his eye out. She started to walk, high stepping for a while until she was sure the creature was out of her way.

She smiled with relief when she realized the boy was Michael.

As usual, he was intent on his images but Cassie was not bothered anymore by that very focused look everyone has here. She walked round to his side of the images to stand beside him. Michael's mouth was tightly closed and his eyes steadfastly remained on his work. He offered no greeting.

"Tony and Douglas have moved to another site," Cassie explained by way of opening the conversation.

"That makes it difficult to understand why you are here. You are missing out on their discoveries." Cassie thought he sounded less than pleased to have her here with him.

"I was distracted at the time," she said.

At this, Michael did turn towards her and looked at her with astonishment.

"Distracted?" He struggled for words. "They were moving on to something more complex and you didn't watch?"

Cassie felt a nudge on her arm. It was like warm fat. She moved her arm and the voice came again, still close by. "You would be with them if you showed interest," it said wetly.

Ignore the creature, Cassie told herself, he is only trying to make her feel terrible and Michael's lack of interest had beaten him to it.

"I want to know where they have gone." She could hear the pleading for help in her voice.

Michael was working his images. "Well, I don't know. Surely you know what they were working on and can figure it out."

"They were working like you," she exclaimed with some frustration, "on explosions and stuff."

Michael looked at her silently. The creature made a slurping sound, maybe it was a chuckle.

Cassie stood straighter and took a deep breath. What were they looking at? She tried to think. Something about blocking, but blocking what and how?

"You should have shown an interest," said a voice from below her.

Maybe she should have been paying more attention. After all, Tony is her brother and staying together is what siblings do. Instead, she had wandered off, talking to everyone else, thinking Tony was being useless by being so intent on his images, when, in actual fact, the images are the ones that will get them home. Did Tony know that? But he didn't want to go home anyhow. Douglas is with him now and he will explain things and help Tony with the necessary images. So she shouldn't worry about Tony. Now, where does she go from here? She doesn't think she knows enough about what Tony and Douglas were exploring to try and follow their thinking.

"You should have paid more attention".

Was that the creature or was she talking out loud? She could feel a thick, damp mess leaning slightly against her leg. She didn't want to look down at it. It was just more horror. She couldn't be enthusiastic about what the boys were creating with their images. It was too loud and always seemed to be on a path of destruction. Their single-minded intent on the images scared her most of all. She did like the colours though, the way they played over everything. And the music. She had heard Michael's beautiful music here.

"Have you written any more music?" she found herself asking.

Michael however, was transfixed by his images and wasn't

listening to her. She repeated the question, louder.

"Haven't you found your own images yet?" Michael enquired dismissively.

"No. I can't and don't want to anyway. How is your music progressing?"

"I cannot create any until I have succeeded with my ideas here."

"Do you reward yourself with the music or are you prevented from playing music when you want to?"

"Of course I can do my music any time I want to," Michael retorted. He waved at his images. "These ideas are very important."

"Can you just play some music now, as background? We would both feel better. It was so beautiful."

Michael's shoulders rose as he sighed deeply. He moved his back towards Cassie which made the images move as well so they were at an angle to Cassie's vision. She became quiet and watched carefully but she could not understand what he was trying to do.

"Do you think he remembers that you are here?" The creature was persisting. She still didn't look for him, hoping his eye had gone back in. She searched Michael's images for signs of music. Maybe he has forgotten she is here. Should she interrupt him again? But he was getting angry with her and he was so little. He seemed to be using all his physical resources dealing with her. What was left looked vulnerable.

"No images, no friends and no brother."

Now Cassie did look down. The creature was right there, beside her, looking up at her, though how she felt that she had no idea as both eyes were hanging out. Its mouth, or mouths, as there were a few of them, were moving around its body, swelling and receding. Suddenly one of the mouths opened and Cassie sensed again, murky fathoms. She smothered a squeal of disgust and quickly closed her own eyes and mouth.

"Will you stop making so much noise," said Michael crossly.

"I'm sorry." Cassie was contrite but also wanted to mention

the creature to see if Michael also sees them. "I keep thinking I see something very ugly. Sometimes it frightens me." She whispered this explanation, not wanting to admit being scared and not wanting the creature to hear her say it.

Michael looked at her. "Have you one of those around?" he asked before returning to his images. Eventually he said, "I don't think I can call up the music. It won't come. I think my mind is too much on my ideas."

Cassie wondered if Michael was prevented from finding his music. Maybe the creature keeps the music away somehow. She kept still as she thought about the creature probably still around her legs. Michael is aware of them.… , she wondered how many there were.

"Maybe," she continued her thoughts aloud, "the music is your connection to your home."

At these words Michael looked around, his eyelight stopping briefly beside her legs.

"The music is mine. It has nothing to do with anything else, except as background to my ideas. It is not important."

They were both silent, then Michael spoke suddenly. "You can see it is not important as your brother is asking for my advice on his engine. It is the ideas that come before everything."

Cassie wondered if she had heard correctly. "My brother?" She went closer to Michaels's images. "Why do you say that?"

"Look," said Michael, pointing at his images, "he has sent his calculations to be checked."

Cassie could see nothing that looked like a calculation. And anyway, why was he working on his engine when he should be trying to find his way home.

"They have got it very wrong," Michael exclaimed, "or maybe their new site is beyond my experiences," he continued in a softer tone. He worked his images. "I will give them what I can." He looked at Cassie. "I will mention that you are well."

"Well! I am not well. Where are these calculations anyway," she demanded.

Michael's finger stirred the images. She could see a few words and then figures. Some she recognized. Maybe she understood the engine better than she realized. The figures coalesced and she saw 17 08 95. Tony's birthday. One of the codes her family used as passwords and pin numbers, her birth date being the other one. But what did it mean? Not much except that maybe Tony and Douglas were trying ways of communicating with her. She couldn't see how it could help but it was comforting.

Images, she needs images to move around and eventually to leave. She doesn't have any interest (which she is sure this world will be able to detect) or knowledge of fireworks to create her own images even if she knew how. She will just have to borrow somebody's for a while. But the same problem exists, she doesn't know enough to be of any use to anybody else and their images. In that case, Cassie told herself, use the knowledge you have. And she does play the flute and she can read music so maybe Michael's music can help her. She won't think about how beautiful it is and therefore how much more complex it is than her renditions of the more popular tunes.

"Michael." As usual, he was engrossed in his images, but Cassie thought she would keep talking, explaining how she wants to go home and the only way is through images. As he has pointed out, she has none. She can't help him with the fireworks but she would be able to understand some of his music. Could he please help her and let her work with him on his music images?

Michael continued working, his face expressionless. He probably didn't hear a word. Cassie sighed and wondered how long she should wait until she tried again. Or was there another way to reach him?

"But you saw," Michael broke the silence, "I cannot go to the music on demand." Cassie looked at him because he sounded sad.

"But maybe I can help. With two of us working the images, our ideas may be strong enough to keep them here."

Michael sat in thought. "I have been trying to produce solo efforts of different instruments to musically charge the fireworks."

"I can do the flute," said Cassie.

Michael looked at her. "Wind, that might work." As he turned back to the images, he moved over so there was room for Cassie. Hardly noting the appearance of a seat for her, Cassie sat down.

Michael started with wind as velocity. The images gusted or swirled and still Cassie could see nothing that looked like music. Instead, the images seemed solid and heavy. Tubes and pellets followed an erratic trajectory, imploding, leaving a heavy, slimy mess that dripped onto the other projectiles. Cassie instinctively ducked as what looked like a miniature torpedo came directly at her.

"Keep concentrating, Cassie," shouted Michael, "the music is there, you need to hear it. Don't be distracted."

She still couldn't understand any of the images so she concentrated on their movements. Make them flow like a tune she thought. But they were resisting. She reluctantly put her fingers in amongst them trying to create rhythms. The pressure on her hands was like the thrashing of a water torrent. She persisted even when she thought something bit her. That couldn't be, but she was hesitant to inspect the now painful finger.

Finally, she heard sound, but how forlorn it was, like wind through the trees when you are lost. The images were following the rhythm of the sound though. There was no discord. Yes, there was, a hum and it was badly out of tune. Something wet smacked against her leg. "You don't understand music if that is all you can create."

That creature again, and now she could hear those jarring notes again. She quickly looked at Michael but nothing had changed there, his images held his attention. Maybe they couldn't do it. The notes rose up around her and they were coming from the direction of the creature. She kicked out where she had last felt him and pushed hard at the images, forcing them into a flowing rhythm,

"I think something is happening!" exclaimed Michael.

The images were changing, as clouds change shape as you watch, and each transformation was a surprise. And then she heard the notes accompanying the movement. They were beautiful, touching her heart, breaking it, except she was smiling. Michael had stopped. Cassie watched his face, relaxed and reflecting the beauty of the music. She realised she hasn't asked him if he wants to come with her if this works.

"Will you come with me Michael, to wherever this music takes us?"

He remained silent and Cassie took that for a yes. How could he not follow? She turned her attention back to the images. She thought she could see an outline of a flute, no, fuller, like a clarinet. A long note issued from it, gathering all the other sounds together so they became a busy background melody to this single note.

"No!" Michael is shouting and she is sitting on the floor.

She swung her eyelight around and there was only empty space.

"He isn't here," she whispered to no one.

"Of course he isn't. The music is not his work." Cassie sagged. The creature had arrived with her. Great. She closed her eyes. "But the music, it was so…it made you happy."

"Not important."

Cassie hugged her knees, squeezing her eyes shut and thought of home and Queenie. How she sits beside Cassie's bed, her big brown, loving eyes watching Cassie wake up and then there is the first bird song of the morning. Cassie and Queenie always share the first light of the morning. Soon they are both outside, running across the field down to the small creek. A kingfisher ceases his search for food and waits on a branch while Cassie throws sticks and wet leaves for Queenie. Their play is joyful and it starts the day.

"What is your problem," she demands of the creature, "and why do you keep following me?"

"You are alone."

"No, I'm not. You are always here." She was cross with him for not being happy company.

Abruptly, the creature was still. All fluid movement ceased. It looked like it had solidified. Cassie's first thought was concern for it but then it started moving again in its peristaltic way. Cassie couldn't help herself, she asked if it was alright.

"I am supposed to be with you," it explained. "Corld insists on it."

Cassie squinted, the creature now blurred in her eyelight. "Is Corld the name of this place?" she asked.

The creature remained silent and his pulsating movements quickened.

"Well,' said Cassie, "at least we know." Opening her eyes wide now, she looked at it for a bit longer, surprising herself that she could. She must be getting used to it.

"My name is Cassie. What is yours?"

The creature looked like it was solidifying again but eventually its voice came from its depths, "I am your thoughts and your torment. There is no name."

"Yes, that may be," said Cassie, "but I can't call you that. How about Seth?"

Now the creature grew and folds of glutinous shine moved around him. His eyes hung down but one raised itself to stare intently at her. His mouths opened into caverns and then closed again, some remaining dark slits that sneered and bubbled. "You cannot call me anything," he slobbered, "I am you, your value."

"Seth it is then," declared Cassie, feeling a secret pleasure in giving him a name since it seemed to make him as uncomfortable as he had made her.

"You will be detected," Seth's voice was suddenly a deep boom.

Cassie moved her eyelight downwards to check Seth's latest mood and configuration but he was nowhere. She swiveled her eyelight, bracing for the shock of suddenly seeing him again, but still nothing. Just as she was getting used to him and now even he has left her by herself. This thought produced a shiver.

Surely not truly alone. This world, Corld, must always have images and boys to keep it going, no matter which site she travels to. With more control, she surveyed the darkness around her. There! She went back and sure enough, there was a boy sitting and looking intently at nothing, just like her first encounter in this place. She looked again, because it wasn't a boy, but a girl. Feeling more positive, Cassie approached the unsuspecting girl.

She stopped beside the girl and looked at her images. Unusually, it was only one image but it took up a lot of space. It was a complexity of shining tubular curves, sometimes a bulging loop with a constellation of small, narrow tubes surrounding it. The twisting form seemed to become lost in its own mass and then suddenly you could glimpse its lines.

"Isn't it the most beautiful musical instrument you ever saw?" exclaimed the girl enthusiastically.

Cassie was relieved not to have had to reveal her ignorance and she studied the image now with this knowledge. It had to be a wind instrument with all those tubes, though she couldn't figure out where the mouthpiece was; maybe it's percussion then. Whatever it was, it was fascinating tracking its multifaceted parts. She said as much to the girl.

The girl was nodding in agreement. "The variety of sounds that come from it is still confusing, but they will be very beautiful."

"So you can make music from it?" asked Cassie.

"Oh yes, wind, and practically an orchestra in itself."

Mindful of where she was, Cassie asked if the girl had created it herself.

"Yes, I did," she answered with wonder in her voice. "I didn't think I would get anywhere near what I could imagine, but it is close. There are some dead spaces still which is wasting breath."

Cassie looked around the site. Her eyelight picked up flows and ripples as if the air in here was visible. She saw two others, definitely boys, at their images and not interested in anything else around them.

"What do you do here?" she asked.

"Create music. But I think there are other things.

Sometimes I see very strange ideas in the air."

Cassie pointed to the image. "Stranger than that? My name is Cassie, by the way."

"Hi." She turned to look at Cassie. "Astrid. Why are you asking? You should know what happens here because you are here."

Cassie sighed and sat down, surprising a seat beside Astrid. "My brother came to this world and I accidently came with him. I do not have my own images."

'Why aren't you with him?"

"I wasn't paying attention and he slipped away to another site."

Astrid stared at her. "He went to another site? What do you mean?"

Cassie wondered where Astrid thought she was. "This place is like a computer with different sites for each subject. You are on the music creation site but if your ideas are better for another subject, you move on to that site." She finished lamely because it sounded weird and Astrid was still staring at her. Slowly, she turned towards her image.

"This has been fun to invent and I don't know I want to go anywhere else after this."

"Where were you before here?" asked Cassie.

Astrid was quiet with thought. Finally she said, "home, I think."

Cassie nodded. "That is where I am trying to go."

"It has been a bit lonely here," Astrid admitted quietly. "You are the first person to talk to me." She gently placed her fingers on her musical instrument and followed the lines of the twists and curves. Minute changes occurred and the instrument did look more efficient. Astrid spoke, her voice alive again. "This is so amazing and I haven't quite finished it. I can't leave it yet." She concentrated on her image and stopped chatting and asking questions.

Cassie realized she had to battle with the lure of the images again. What is it about them? No one can hold a thought that doesn't involve their images. Douglas did say this world prevented thinking. Maybe it is not only the lure of the images that does this but this world doesn't let them think about the outside. Cassie sat still. That would mean this world could block thoughts. No, not block thoughts, but keep the ideas focused by not allowing any interaction with other people or beings. Maybe this world is as small as Tony's bedroom after all and it only seems bigger because of the world of information the computer contains. It's not big enough to run with Queenie though.

"What will you do with the instrument when you have finished it?" asked Cassie.

"I don't know." Astrid was sounding irritable, just like Michael when Cassie kept interrupting him. "Probably try and make it."

"I don't think you can make a physical thing in this world," Cassie was thinking aloud.

"Of course you can," declared Astrid, "otherwise what would be the point."

"But it doesn't work like that. It only progresses ideas it wants to, and I don't think an instrument that plays beautiful music is part of that."

Astrid was looking at Cassie now. "It must want beautiful music, otherwise, I repeat, what is the point of my instrument?"

"I don't know. Maybe it is the ideas that come about while you are creating the instrument that are useful. The instrument itself is not important. Unless of course it can be used for causing hurt and damage. That is what is encouraged here."

Astrid looked at her instrument again. "I can't believe it is that bad here. But if it is so, where could I go from here?"

Cassie tried to make sense of the sites. "I came here through music. Michael was trying for a unique sound through a single instrument. So here I am, where you create sounds and their instruments."

Astrid wasn't convinced. "That doesn't sound evil at all. More like an incoherent idea."

"Maybe, but I don't think your instrument will be played as you imagine it. Maybe it won't be played at all."

Astrid thought about this. "No music or lots of instruments

that cannot make a sound."

"Or," said Cassie, "a sound you never want to hear."

"Now that is a nightmare site," remarked Astrid. "But Cassie, you can't really believe this world is like that. The music here is beautiful. And what were you creating when you arrived here?"

Astrid was right. It was Michael's astonishing music. She did travel on that.

"And you still do not know what it means or how to find your brother."

Cassie looked up in surprise. They were harsh words but Astrid was busy with her instrument. A slimy warmth pressed against her leg and she looked down at Seth. He was leaning against the bench, both eyes dangling over the edge. The mouth on his back was doing the talking. "You will never find Tony, you will miss each other continually."

The voice knew about this world and Cassie felt the hollow feeling of doubt. She continued to look at him, trying to see something positive. Seth's eyes were slowly retracting but his mouths were getting in the way, preventing the eyes from settling into their proper places. If they even have a socket for them, thought Cassie. They ogled and swung about amongst the moving lips and suddenly the eyes were amongst the folds of Seth's skin. Cassie wondered if he ever accidently swallowed one of his eyes.

"How can I get home?" she found herself asking.

All Seth's mouths slid into grins. "You need to be useful here," he said.

"Useful?" shouted Cassie, "useful to who? This place? And then it will let me go because it benefits from my being here? Don't talk nonsense, Seth."

"You will have images if you are useful." The grins were fixed, despite some swelling of his body and his eyes rolling around as if they wanted to escape their sockets again.

Cassie slowly reached out a finger towards Seth. She felt a pressure as if she had knocked the tip of her finger hard against a solid object. Gradually it became too painful and she curled her fingers into a protective fist. "Aren't you an image? Maybe my image?"

One eyeball did pop out. "I have explained." Seth was irritated. "I am the potential and the wrong turning." The loose eyeball watched her closely. "You do not listen or understand. No wonder you are on your own always." Seth peeled himself away from the seat and moved into the darkness.

"If you had your own images, you would not have to talk to yourself about your ideas."

With a start, Cassie remembered Astrid. "Sorry Astrid, but there is a creature that keeps appearing, an ugly little thing. Do you ever see anything like that?"

Astrid was looking at Cassie with concern. "Sometimes, but only very quickly and always somewhere else. Certainly, I wouldn't want to talk to them."

Cassie didn't know what to do. Everyone she met gave the opinion she wasn't doing the right thing here. She watched Astrid's instrument glow with colour. "Tell me about your instrument."

Astrid was immediately animated and launched into chatter. "Here is where you blow," she began.

Even with it pointed out to her, Cassie couldn't picture it, but she didn't interrupt.

"It is quite easy really." Astrid's fingers moved around the instrument and suddenly it was a bit bigger and revolving slowly, stopping or moving quicker at the commands of Astrid's fingers.

Cassie was entranced, she was also beginning to see how it could work. Astrid continued, manipulating the instrument the whole time.

"The keys here, nearest the mouthpiece, not only make notes but pump the air along. This one here can also pump in extra air through the mouthpiece. It requires precision timing or your lips get sucked in." Astrid was hardly stopping for air herself and Cassie thought it was marvelous.

"See here, the curve and circumference of these tubes produce these notes." A trilling melody started somewhere, like panpipes, but with an echo. "Then here," Astrid's fingers were busy at the top of the instrument, "this noise." A bass note sounded that gathered strength before it stopped suddenly." Astrid was busy further along the instrument. "Here, there is an accumulation of dead air and I have to fix that."

Cassie was studying the weave of the instrument.

"You know Astrid, this is basically the same principles my brother was working with for his explosions and where the sound would go. I think working on the dead air may take us somewhere."

Astrid stopped working and looked at Cassie. "Where?"

"I don't know."

Astrid enlarged the loops of the instrument where the air tended to settle. "Instead of increasing the force to move the air, I can change the loops so the air cannot settle. It could bounce off the sides, creating its own momentum."

Cassie thought it all sounded familiar. As Astrid worked, small pulsations shifted the air around the instrument. Small pockets of air seemed to swell until it looked as if it would split open but then would deflate just in time. Cassie placed her finger onto the next swelling, wondering what she would see if the air did rupture the instrument. It was like touching thick honey. Colours appeared where her finger intruded on the bulge. She moved her finger, creating swirls of color and mass. Cassie was beginning to understand the enchantment of the images. They seemed to contain another dimension just behind everything. Moving her arm, she could imagine it was going through other places. Different sensations tingled on her skin. What would happen to noise if Tony's engine could break through these swellings?

Astrid was laughing. "If that instrument can make a noise, you are better at this than me," she exclaimed.

Cassie looked at the images. While she had been thinking, she had doodled something out of the colour and mass that looked something like Tony's noise engine, except she had given it a form that would not render explosions but more of a *phut.*

Cassie also had to laugh. The body of the engine was rotund, a tube wound itself round that and thinner lines crisscrossed over it.

"It looks like a fat emu moving its neck to peer everywhere at once," Astrid managed to say between giggles.

"Probably more like that than Tony's engine," Cassie agreed.

"So maybe we can perfect it," said Astrid.

They were busy, first trying to figure out where they could introduce any means to make noise.

"What about here," asked Cassie, rotating the image slowly. She concentrated as the tube changed position as the body revolved. "Maybe the sound could change through its physical position rather than the internal workings. That would be baffling, as everyone playing it would have a different perception of the same instrument."

Astrid was thoughtful. "That could help move my dead air. A metal that can be softened briefly to push the air along."

"I can make you that metal." Both girls jumped, noticing the head that had come between them and was studying their images.

Cassie looked at Astrid but she shook her head. Cassie wondered if they had moved sites. But it was difficult to tell when the intense faces at the images all looked the same and darkness enveloped anything else.

"It's strange seeing girls here, especially two, but I can show you the ropes." He looked expectantly at Astrid, then turned to Cassie and just watched her.

"Hi, I'm Cassie and this is Astrid. Where are we?"

"Not usually asked that question. Can't get anyone to say anything when they first arrive. Too busy working their images." He looked at Cassie with suspicion before turning to Astrid.

"You are at a metal properties site. I stretch all sorts of metal, works like plasticene, acts like metal. It can fool the eye." He winked at Astrid.

"How come you are not working your images?" asked Cassie.

"New people are just as interesting," he replied, smiling.

"Besides, I have been investigating this place, figuring out how it works."

Cassie wondered how much he did know. He seemed a boastful sort of fellow, usually a sign of not much knowledge and he hasn't even given his name yet.

"Have you been to any other site?" Cassie asked.

He hesitated briefly, looking a bit surprised. It was possibly a new idea for him but he replied by asking them a question.

"What site have you come from?"

Astrid interrupted, impatient to find out if he can solve the problem of her instrument. "It was a musical site, but look here. This is how I want my instrument to act, just here." She turned to him, "What is your name again?"

"Nevin."

"Nevin, good." Astrid started on a detailed description of how she wants her instrument to work. Eventually he stops her flow by confidently declaring he can fix it.

"But how did you get here?" he finished.

Astrid turned to Cassie and Nevin also expectantly faced her.

"Well, if your idea progresses to beyond what the site can offer, sometimes you can move to another site that can help."

Nevin pointed to the images. "There is only one. Whose images are they?"

"Mine," said Astrid. "Cassie has never had her own but is trying to get home through them." She looked at Cassie. "Is that right?"

"Yes, it is."

Nevin was staring intently at her. She thought his interest was strange for this world. Why wasn't he engrossed in his own images? She decided she wouldn't add that to her other worries. Metal, where could she go with metal? Douglas had an interest in that somehow. Maybe she could find Tony and Douglas through here. But they would be moving too, whereas home is stationary. It is probably best to keep heading for home.

While Cassie was trying to plan the next move, Astrid and Nevin were working on her instrument, though Nevin stopped now and then to ask Cassie questions on where she had been and who she had met. But Astrid always drew him back with her enthusiasm. The pull of the images was strong and Cassie noted it again as Nevin was easily distracted from his questions to help Astrid with his metals. He was as enthusiastic about his ideas as Tony or Michael had been over their images. But Nevin was showing a lot of interest in her and what she had been doing.

"Have you tried to go home?" Cassie asked suddenly.

He looked at Cassie as if he had been expecting the question.

"I thought of it, which made me look closer at where I was and how the place worked. I have a few ideas on how to move around but I do not want to leave yet."

"What are your ideas? How do you think it is possible to leave here?" Cassie was eager, forgetting any suspicions she may have had about Nevin.

Nevin thought for a while. "No, I think connections through images are the best way. But you need your own."

Cassie deflated. There was nothing new about that opinion.

"But Cassie," Astrid sounded concerned, "you know you can use mine."

Nevin interrupted to add another idea to the instrument and very quickly, both were busy expanding this new thought.

Cassie watched her animal in the corner. It certainly looked more like an emu now than a machine. It was slowly revolving, trying out all the positions from which it could make noise. It seemed to like the noise when it was on its back. It was a low melodious note but when the creature stretched its tube, (it does look like a neck, thought Cassie), the note turned into a pro-longed metal tinkle. Cassie helped the creature to turn and so she could hear all its noises. Suddenly she realized the creature was prompting her. She knew which way he wanted to turn and she couldn't do anything else but help him. She wondered if this was another way this place worked, pushing a particular idea.

Astrid sat back, pleased with the way her instrument was working out.

"I may be able to perfect it before we move on," she

informed Cassie.

"That's great, Astrid, because I think a connection through your metal will be easy to find."

Nevin turned to her. "These are my ideas. They cannot go anywhere else."

"Don't be silly, Nevin," said Astrid, "that is what this place is, the expansion of ideas."

"No." Nevin's tone was softer but still assured. "The dimensions and calculations are only for your instrument. They will not work with anything else."

Astrid ignored this because she was keen to return to the instrument. "We have nearly finished Cassie, then we will be able to work something out."

Cassie smiled at her. After all, they were Astrid's images. Cassie couldn't force her to think going home was a better idea than her instrument and Nevin seemed to be a great help.

Cassie wondered why she couldn't work up the same enthusiasm for the images. She watched her little animal and its efforts to make different noises. Every now and then a beautiful noise reached her ears but she wasn't sure from which image it came. She touched her image again to help him, then stopped. No, she thought, she would hinder him and see what happens. The image swelled as he fought against her ideas for him. Cassie was thinking he wasn't looking so cute anymore. He was big now, bigger than the other images. In fact, there were no images. No Astrid or Nevin either. Her emu creature was moving away, his neck trying to untwist as he went and Seth was standing next to her. His mouths were set in many drooling lines and his eyes in place though still looking in different directions.

"You cannot do it. You cannot pay attention and show an interest. Now you have lost your new companions." Both Seth's eyes focused on her. "And the images, gone again."

Cassie looked around and could see it was true. There were no images here. Well there were, but they were not being worked, they were walking around, many bigger than her. They looked menacing in their silent wanderings. But they did change and she tried to figure out how they were being changed, who was adjusting them. Then she saw them. Children, very small children, four, five, six years old, gleefully following the creatures around, sometimes sitting with them. They poked their fingers into the creatures and the changes happened.

She turned to Seth. "Children, you bring children here?"

Seth's mouths moved, but he said nothing.

Bella

Bella felt herself being pulled aside. She tried to remember why this should happen but gave up as soon as she remembered she was in the computer. Who knows why anything happens in here, she thought. Bill Gates may not even comprehend all that he has unleashed. Something was definitely preventing her from going onward. It wasn't anything solid, just a heavy presence that was restraining her. *Therefore* probably got himself into trouble again causing 3 to stop the compulse .

She felt the quiet around her, just as if no one was there. She looked around in a slight panic which made her feel nauseous. There was something wrong with her vision. A big block of colour with words was in front of her but it was distorted as if seeing it through cracked glass. She turned her head at angles and rubbed her eyes, but nothing made a difference. The atmosphere itself appeared to be displaced, particles seeming to be in different dimensions. She wondered if continually using a computer or in her case, being in one, was indeed bad for the eyesight. Through all this, she couldn't distinguish any other beings with her. She called out for 3 or Grease and *therefore.* Spotting three mobile dots in this place would be impossible though. Nothing answered and she couldn't feel any reassuring touch on her knees.

She stepped forward and found her movements were heavy. This site was not a healthy place to be but she didn't know how to leave or indeed, why she was here at all. That is what she would concentrate on, finding out about this site.

Bella sat down facing the coloured wall. It was a relief to be able to do something without effort, even if it was only the simple act of sitting. Now, to try and decipher her surroundings. She stared at the wall with its writing. If she moved her eyes slowly, she found she could see individual letters, though it was making her eyes water. There was an 'n' and an 'o.' The first word was 'no' and now that she could make it out, it was standing out boldly. Not a promising start to any message, but in keeping with the atmosphere of this place. The concentration to read other words was intense; her head swam with the effort, and her eyes were starting to hurt. Bella calmed down, telling herself to slow down again. It was a familiar text and she wondered why, before suddenly remembering where she was. Of course, it was a computer text, one of those annoying messages that pop up telling you there can be no connection to the site requested and to try again or access 'help.' The longer she looked though, the more the letters seemed to throb, causing the letters to move closer to her before receding and to be replaced by others. And the letters were not placed properly. Sometimes she didn't recognize the word but it was there, big and bold in front of her, demanding to be accepted as law. They threatened. No sites are accessible, according to the words and there is no help. Bella looked around, forgetting about her nausea in her growing unease. There still was nothing else to look at, just crooked and disturbing emptiness.

There should be a way out, after all it was a computer. It is just a matter of knowing and then she stupidly frightened herself with the thought it was all probably beyond her knowledge of how to work a computer. If she weren't in it, she would have just turned the computer off, waited a couple of minutes before turning it on again. But living in a computer was different. Could she work it out or was she just a bit in the computer at the mercy of its inexplicable workings? She was paralyzing herself with her assumed inadequacies. No doubt this is how some youngsters feel in social and family situations. Maybe that is why they spend so much time at their computers. A blue intense light sparked near the wall of text and travelled along the broken paths of her vision. It jumped at the bends, the blue condensing into a brilliance that hurt her eyes. She instinctively shut her eyes but opened them quickly so as not to be caught off guard by what may happen next. And it was a monstrosity that had partially oozed through the wall of text. It was looking at her though she couldn't discern any eyes, but its attention, she felt sure, was on her. It dribbled a thick substance that also contained small solid bits. As it moved to come further through the wall, a spurt of this fluid came for her. Bella threw herself sideways and tried to regain her feet. Where it wasn't dribbling, it bubbled, and now and then a bubble would turn into a shiny orb that looked smooth and clean like an over inflated balloon, especially when compared to the rest of it. Then one burst.

Bella was thankful her vision was distorting the creature, being bent into hundreds of parts made it more abstract than real.

"We could feel you here," a voice resonated through the site.

Bella was still, hoping 3 would appear, his reassuring presence standing tall beside her knee. But there was only this gruesome image at the wall and herself.

"What is this place?" she asked.

"What it is does not concern you. That you are here is unlikely," the voice replied.

Ongoing conversation on Bella's part was hindered by her unwillingness to display her lack of knowledge and helplessness. Her hesitation was filled by the voice.

"Who helped you here?"

"It was an accident," Bella replied. "Why do you want to know?"

Another spray of fluid splashed around her as the creature squirmed again. Some of it landed on her arm. It felt warm and she tried not to think about it. Was the creature trying to get through to this place? She decided to keep talking to distract it from this effort. I am in a computer, she reminded herself so keep the conversation restricted to whole concepts rather than ambiguous questions like 'What is going on?' which is all she wanted to know.

"The boys here…," she faltered. How many words is too long? The apparition became still, even its dribbling seemed to freeze.

"The boys are making their ideas!" it finally boomed.

Bella felt a surge of relief she was still somehow near everything else this world contained. What does this creature do here? she wondered.

"Job of…?" She hesitated again, not knowing what to call him though in her world he would be a monster. She finished with that.

It became still again, (maybe that is how it thinks, Bella figured) and a long dribble extension cracked and fell to the floor. The shiny orbs grew, stretching their outer coverings and the shine dulled to opaque. More words appeared on the red wall. It was vexing having to be so slow at reading the words. 'Ideas,' 'little boys,' 'Saedi,' 'destroy' and others she was too impatient to comprehend. But because she was concentrating so intensely, she realized 'Saedi' was 'ideas' backwards. She wondered if this was relevant. She said the word aloud, hoping her pronunciation, as in Sadie the cleaning lady, was correct.

"I am a Saedi," the creature cried, spurting fluid.

"Your job?" repeated Bella.

"Saedi directs the boys."

"To where?" asked Bella.

"To what Corld wants," the Saedi answered simply.

"What is that?"

"The world and all its opportunities." The red wall changed. It had become a kaleidoscope of images. She saw elephants and bears, sunrises glowed and dimmed into sunsets, changing the lights and colours of the passing scenes. The beauty of the earth with all of its complicated relations was a moving picture in the red wall. Bella smiled, remembering her travels and the special encounters with people and animals that gave her inspiration and courage. Technology entered the images but seemed to compliment nature's work.

"The boys can imagine and create anything they want. It is

all here." The voice penetrated into Bella's memories.

"No," she replied, "it is not all there. Where are the smells, the interaction, the challenge of being a part of the environment?"

The images faded but the Saedi was no longer in the wall. Words had replaced him.

> **The boys want to be here.**
> **Leave them alone.**

Reading them, Bella began to wonder if it was true. Everything here seemed to be beyond her comprehension and the boys here must be enjoying the technological challenges. But Corld is not the only place that can provide that challenge. Imaginations and skills can be stretched in many ways. One place does not have exclusive rights to learning. Her fractured vision caught a movement. The Saedi was coming back. Blinking away the tears of concentration, Bella stared at the wall. A number three emboldened itself through the wall then plopped down, laying flat on the floor.

Bella moved towards it. It must be her 3, she thought. 3, grease and *therefore* are the only consistent things in this place. As she neared, the 3 became upright, shook itself and came towards her.

"You are safe," he stated.

"Yes. It is good to see you again. What happened?" replied Bella, not knowing the etiquette of showing fondness towards a number.

"We sensed you were not with us and all this time we have been trying to return to you." 3 became still. "We were in Corld."

"Where are Grease and *therefore*?"

"Still there, trying to return here."

"What is preventing their return?" Bella dared to ask.

"In Corld, we were part of the boys' ideas, part of their images. That must be why you couldn't follow us." 3 swiveled round. "This place must be between Corld and our proper site."

If that was the case, Bella thought, and it seems likely, she must find a way to be part of the images. She knows a Saedi now and wondered if who you knew was important here.

3 continued, interrupting her thoughts. "We experimented with removing ourselves from their images and found it to be easy, so we explored further, travelling through the evolving ideas. But the ideas are being channeled towards self-centered interests of Corld, which seems to mostly involve the perpetuation of power through coercion and might. The ideas Corld are encouraging are destructive and ultimately dominant. Not all the boys want their ideas to progress this way but Corld can manipulate the progression so it seems like it is the only way the ideas can go forward."

"The same tactics as in any misinformation," murmured Bella.

3 stretched up in enquiry but continued. "It was more difficult to remove ourselves from this level. We were being mangled to fit this erroneous shape of the idea. Our meaning was being warped and we were losing our sense of it."

Another spurt of fluid hit Bella. She instinctively jumped back, falling over in the disorientation of her vision.

Grease loomed over her. "I am sorry," he said, falling back into a harmless lump.

"It is good you are here," Bella assured him with happy relief. "Now we must wait for *therefore*."

"No," Grease was adamant, "he is in Corld and has found a passage through which Bella, you can follow."

Bella had to keep moving her head to find the best angle to view Grease and 3 as they spoke of their adventures. The effort of looking brought tears to her eyes and she had to keep wiping them

"It is through the ideas, the images," 3 explained. "The boys, and we assume you as well, need your own images to be drawn into Corld and the development of the ideas allows the boys to travel through Corld."

"*Therefore* found a fault in one of the pathways," continued grease. "Somebody has found a way to link incompatible channels and he is keeping these open by producing consequences. We should go now," he finished.

"Ready Bella?" asked 3.

"Yes." Anything, she thought, to rid herself of this fractious vision.

Tony, Douglas, Ned and Ben

"Ned's right, it does stink here," remarked Douglas, "I wonder why."

Tony had moved away from them and was wandering around and through the images, his face a picture of delight.

Douglas, Ned and Ben could only stare. There was so much activity. Roving eyelights lit up the whole site. Boys were actively working their images and they were calling to each other. The place was crowded with people, movement and interaction.

"This is not right," said Douglas. "They seem to be sharing and talking with each other."

"And it still smells," added Ned.

Tony returned, his eyelight shining bright and picking them out easily. "This is fantastic. These fellows have finished their ideas. That guy there," he pointed to a boy nearby, slowly revolving his images, smiling hugely, "has created solid sound waves. You can see the music." Tony fell silent, then started his excited chatter again. "I could use that for some of my fireworks effects." He turned to his engine, sitting again next to Ben. "This is so different to the music site, Ben. Your mind must have taken us far away."

"No Tony, I think it was only one very small step backwards," replied Ben, looking around.

Douglas nudged Tony. "Some of these boys don't look as happy as your friend."

"They are just fine tuning," answered Tony. "That's what

this is, the achievement site. They are proud of their ideas."

"And where do these boys go now?" asked Ben.

Tony became still. Ned shifted, unsure if he should fill the silence and Douglas continued looking around with his eyelight. Finally, Tony spoke, nearly whispering.

"I don't know Ben. What happens to them now?"

"Do you know," said Douglas, "I think there are other creatures here." He paused. "They seem to be interacting with the boys somehow."

At the same time, Ned was remarking on the boys' behaviour. "They look upset and scared more than elated," he said.

Tony was watching the boy with the solid sound and he was no longer smiling with success, but working rapidly on his images and looking very distressed.

With so much activity, it was difficult to understand exactly what was happening. Tony was right, thought Ben, this is an achievement site, but there is no place for stopping in Corld. Ideas must change and continue on. And this site is what happens when the boys' ideas are completed. Corld has had the boys focused on one ending. Alternatives were not encouraged and their ability to think beyond boundaries has shrunk and now they cannot think at all. "What Ned can smell is the decay of ideas," said Ben. "If the boys cannot come up with new and different ways of thinking, the images cannot be used and they decompose. That is what this activity is, not boys progressing their ideas, but boys trying to prop up stagnant ones."

Tony looked at his engine and then turned his eyelight to the frenzy of activity around him. "This must be hell for them," he said.

"It is no doubt," agreed Ben, "and if their minds cannot turn to new ideas, the only way they can move out of it, is to not think at all."

Tony looked at Ben. "The dead music site."

"Certainly a dead site." Ben thought for a bit. "And Corld must have dead sites relating to every concept that is being progressed in this world because everything can come to an end."

Douglas listened to these exchanges, waiting for Ben to explain these other creatures wandering around, but he was still pondering the existence of the numerous sites where there is nothing. Douglas caught a memory of the boys at the dead music site. There is nothing else in Corld except thought, so take away the ideas that form the boys and…he didn't want to think about it.

His eyelight caught out one of the creatures. It wasn't human and it was talking to another creature but they were very different from each other. They seemed to be discussing the dilemmas of the boys. One of them approached a boy, but the boy hardly takes any notice, again because of his concern for his images.

"Hester once said there was something dangerous about this place." Ned was beside him, adding his eyelight to the two creatures. "Do you think it has something to with those guys?"

"I don't know." He remembered the friend or fiend in the message from Michael. "I hope not as I think Cassie may have met one."

"They could be Hester's monsters. You have been in more places here, have you seen them before?" asked Ned.

"No, I haven't."

"I wonder why Cassie would have seen one then," mused Ned. "I suppose there is only one way to find out." With that, he walked over to the two creatures in his eyelight.

Douglas felt obliged to follow, especially when one of the creatures turned his attention onto Ned and kept it there as he approached.

The creature grew as Ned came closer. It loomed as a deep purple mass sending out blinding flashes that tore at its shape. It moved as if these hurt and bits fell off it now and then. It restored one bit to its shape, presumably by suction, and loomed above Ned again. He couldn't tell if it had a head or not, it was just a glutinous shape. Then suddenly, it produced a mouth.

"Your images, go to them!" a voice slowly enunciated.

Ned looked to the other creature in between the blinding

flashes as that is where the voice came from. It was off putting as the purple creature was the only one that was studying him.

"He doesn't have images," Douglas announced. Ned tried to catch Douglas' eye, wondering if this is the sort of information these creatures should be made aware of. "Why do images matter to you?" Douglas asked.

The creatures had somehow moved closer to Douglas and Ned, the purple creature spreading a bright aura that hovered menacingly. What could be called eyes stared at them. It was difficult not to stand still under that glare as the probable eyes were circular balls, multi faceted and multi coloured, and they rolled around and sometimes broke away and moved around the creature's shape.

Ned decided bravado was his only option. No images," he confirmed, "I am here, doing nothing."

Lights flashed and Ned winced because it looked like the eyes were burning up. Both creatures then straightened and looked at each other. As the fire subsided, they slowly turned to face Douglas and Ned. There was silence as each twosome tried to comprehend what was before them. Finally a voice from the creatures spoke.

"And they are still here."

"Of course we are still here," said Ned. "Corld is not all powerful after all."

The two creatures visibly stiffened. "You will go away eventually," one said, "probably very unpleasantly."

The purple creature turned back to the boy in front of them. The other creature had no recognizable features so there was no way of knowing where he was facing or even if he was the right side up. Meantime, the boy was oblivious to the four beings beside him. His movements were rapid and his concentration was solely on trying, desperately, to hold his idea together. A protuberance emerged from the purple mass and he waved it round in front of the boy. "Your idea could be used for the flexibility of sound waves. Look over there." A thick mass of purple mingled around the deteriorating image and then moved away in the direction of another boy. Douglas and Tony were mesmerized by the dissolving but forever moving purpleness. It was the movement of cloud, rolling into its own mass as it drifted away. But the boy was paying as little attention to that as he was to anything else that wasn't his image.

"It's hopeless isn't it?" the boy whispered. Douglas was about to answer. No, it wasn't hopeless, he could see how the image could merge with sound waves, but another voice came first.

"The boy is not going to change his idea," it said. Ned looked and the other creature had turned into an elongated form of a person. His colour was a mustard yellow though the shade changed as it bulged in places. There was no rhythm to it and sometimes a reasonable replica of human arms and legs would appear. Flecks of his substance kept falling off as well, but he ignored them. "It was a good idea. You progressed it expertly and we did have fun moving through the nuclear debris."

The purple mass quivered. Douglas wondered if the creatures could laugh.

"We nearly lost the idea then. The shapes the images produced were unsightly and that horrible noise persisted." The purple mass was still. "Do you have a child yet?" he asked of his fellow creature.

The elongated creature turned to Douglas and Ned and suddenly it was standing before them.

"Where are your ideas?" the creature demanded.

"In here," said Ned, pointing to his head. The creature brought his upper torso closer and moved around Ned's head. "What do they look like?"

Ned could feel the warm dampness of a swamp moving around him and that smell was lingering. He became still with thought. "I don't know yet, but Corld makes mistakes." Ned held out his arms. "I shouldn't be here so there are unstable areas which could be influenced. What it would look like I can't imagine yet. But once started, it could go in any direction you wanted." He came to and looked at the creature still close to him, this one produced eyes that were shining and excreting a slimy mess. "Just like hacking and it should be easier as I am in the site already." He smiled at the creature.

The creature opened a cavernous mouth, too deep for the head, but Douglas got in first. "Do you hack?"

"Not very well," Ned replied. "But I enjoy finding out what machines can be capable of. Because computers haven't been around that long, their history is interesting. Hacking is an important part of that as the hackers are most times the catalyst for another stage of development. It is the curiosity they have for what computers, or originally any type of machine, can actually achieve. So they explore. Just working with computers cannot give you that knowledge."

The mouth of the creature closed but the line bent in the middle. Ned wasn't sure if it was a smile or a sneer.

"Change Corld?" a contemptuous snort came from the creature but it wasn't a sound. It was as if the question had been writ in large, pulsating letters and hung for all to see. Ned didn't know where to look. But the purple creature came close, his words slurred and bubbled, "What do you mean change Corld? Corld changes all the time because it is about ideas. They are given the opportunity to grow and develop."

"In all directions or in just the one according to what Corld wants?" asked Ned.

The creatures' movements increased. It reminded Ned of how Tony's engine bucked and swelled. They looked like they could explode. He hoped not, there was sure to be a smell and it would be worse than the lingering decay he could still detect.

"You have irritated them." Douglas was fascinated. These creatures were considering what Ned had been saying. They were paying attention, but why? This place was theirs. It was Ned and Douglas who were the interlopers and not conforming to Corld. So why were these monsters paying attention at all.

Finally, the elongated creature curved towards Ned. "We progress or there is nothing else."

Douglas glanced at the crumbling image and back to the festering bodies of these creatures. These creatures reflect what is happening to everything in this site. It is falling apart. There is no progression of ideas here. Maybe that is why these creatures look like they are decomposing, because they are—because they are the ideas. Douglas wondered if that made sense. It didn't, but in Corld, it could do.

Ned waved his arms, trying to encompass all he could not express. "There is always more. Every idea has an opposite or an alternative that can take it in other directions."

The creature swayed its head towards the boy still trying to put together his image. "Did you hear that?" the creature asked of the boy, "you can change."

The purple creature became blinding to the eye, his purple colouring disappearing in his brightness.

"No, he can't Pastel." He waved protuberances at the elongated creature. "He doesn't want to. He will lose his idea if he does and that is the only one he has."

"But I am his idea!" Pastel cried out, growing longer until he was more like a confused stick figure. "But," he swung around Ned like a python, "this boy thinks I can become alternatives. So I am more than those images." Pastel's head spun a bit more round Ned so the globes, still weeping, were staring into Ned's eyes. "Is that not so," he demanded.

Ned wanted to agree just so Pastel would free him but he had not understood anything. Douglas, to Ned's consternation, wasn't helping but quietly thinking while walking towards the purple creature. "Are you the physical embodiments of the ideas of the boys?" he asked.

"Greater than the ideas, we are the potential in the ideas. We guide the boys and their ideas through Corld." He turned, flashing purple at Pastel. "How can we be an idea that doesn't exist?"

"But Peter," said Pastel, slowly releasing Ned, "you just said we are the potential. That is something that doesn't exist."

"Yes it does, it is in there, in the boys' ideas."

Douglas tried not to wonder how the purple monstrosity could be called Peter and concentrated on the discussion.

"But it doesn't have to end here," persisted Pastel.

"Yes it does, because Corld wanted that idea to progress like it has," Peter replied. He stopped and looked at Douglas and Ned, his brightness diminished. "Is that what you mean? An idea Corld doesn't want might continue on?"

Douglas smiled. "That is it exactly and if Corld tested the other ideas, it would change Corld."

Peter was twisting back and forth. "That wouldn't work. If Corld doesn't know it, there are no images and the images are necessary. We would end up like Seth. He is trying to control a girl who does not have ideas. She is a danger and Seth is losing his purpose."

Douglas stared at him and Peter's eyes grew and slithered around his mass but always looking at Douglas. He finally demanded, "How do you know these ideas exist if there are no images for them?"

Douglas went closer to Peter. "The other ideas do exist or why else would this girl be a danger. Where is she? We can help you with her."

Pastel swung his orbs back to Ned. "You can use this boy's images for your ideas. Let me help you."

"But those images are at their end," said Ned.

"That's right," agreed Douglas. "Tell us more about what Seth is doing to control this girl. Maybe he has found a way to start images."

"No," Peter was shaking his purple body, bits flying off as he did so. "We do not create these images. Corld brings them to us. We only facilitate them."

"But," Douglas continued doggedly, "if you discovered new ideas, surely you could see them and create their likeness in the images."

Peter and Pastel looked at each other. They mumbled to each other. "Seth is trying."

"Yes, but look at the state he is in."

"Corld will notice soon and call him back."

"Maybe he is succeeding."

"He is unresponsive to our questions."

A sigh seemed to come from Pastel. "I will have to go back to the small ones."

Peter moved his eyes so one held Douglas in his glare and the other held Ned. "Other ideas cannot be done here. Pastel will continue with this image and you," a quivering mess of purple reached out for Ned, "will work it."

Ned was still puzzling over Pastel's remark. "Who are the small ones?"

Pastel looked bored now. "They are Corld's future, if we can direct their ideas. It is not easy, they are inconclusive."

"Where is the girl who is with Seth," Douglas demanded.

Peter turned and fixed his gaze onto Douglas. "The best way to find her is through this image."

"No we won't, this image will only work for Corld's ideas, not for ours." Douglas grabbed hold of Ned's arm and pushed him away. "Let's find Tony and Ben."

Ned was being dragged forward purposely by Douglas while also trying to get his bearings by his eyelight. It was not working. "Where are Tony and Ben?"

"I don't know," said Douglas, "but we had to get away. The images are dangerous. They make you forget everything else and those creatures know how to make you work them."

Ned looked around. "I don't think we have to move so fast. Peter and Pastel are right beside us."

Douglas also looked and sure enough, there they were, keeping pace and concentrating on the two boys. "I guess you are right, Ned. This place is a computer site. I mean, where do you go to get away from anyone."

Douglas carefully scanned the place with his eyelight. "There they are." He nodded, pointing in the direction with his eyelight. "With that boy and his images. Just as well Ben is there with Tony. Tony gets too excited about these things. Come on."

As they approached, they could hear Tony talking earnestly to the boy. The boy was very busy with his image and didn't seem to be paying attention to Tony's words. Ben was quietly standing nearby, listening, or he may have been asleep. It was difficult to tell.

"But you have to change it," they could hear Tony exclaiming, probably not for the first time.

"Leave me alone! It is a good idea." The boy's tone was harsh.

Ned stared at Douglas. "Tony has got the boy talking," he said with wonder.

"I wouldn't get too excited. I think Tony has just annoyed him into a reaction. I don't think it is a conversation."

Tony was staring at the images with the helplessness of loss. "You are right, it is a good idea and you have made it work. But this perfection only lasts a split second because everything changes and your idea has to change as well, otherwise it becomes useless." Tony watched another piece of the image dislodge itself. "And eventually dies," he added.

The boy rushed to replace the broken area of his image. Tenderly, he worked it to smooth out the edges but nothing could disguise the continual erosion of the image. He replaced more rotten areas. All his energy and attention was on the futile repair of his idea.

Tony turned to face everyone. "This is horrible. A nightmare. This must be Corld's hell, where all your energy is spent glorifying an idea that goes nowhere."

"Yes Tony." Ben was standing straighter, also watching the boy's efforts. "And the nightmare ends when you are silent. The fear of change keeps you active, ensuring there is no change. But that is a way to madness and the only way to cope with change when you fear it, is to stay still and be nothing. Like the dead music site."

"I am not going back there," Ned said adamantly.

"But there is no risk of that is there?" asked Tony. "There are ideas here, plenty of images. How can Corld take away their minds?"

"There is no real thinking in Corld, Tony." Ben waved his arms around. "Look at them all here. They each have one idea, maybe they were great ideas even. But nothing grows in a vacuum. There is no interaction with other minds, there are no distractions, no interruptions from mothers calling you to the delicious smells of dinner. You don't go outside to listen to birds or admire the scenery. You don't argue with your friends and you certainly never have to consider the consequences of your ideas. Corld reduces your minds. There is no real challenge here." Ben stared at them. They stared back but only momentarily. They fidgeted and looked around. Finally, Tony's eyelight returned to Ben.

"Right, so what do we do now, Ben?"

"Grab any image and start working it."

"But we don't know what these ideas are," said Tony, though he didn't sound upset by this thought.

"You can't help yourself can you Tony?" remarked Douglas. "Even after everything we are beginning to understand, you still want to have your images."

"Yes, I do," Tony agreed, "but not for ever. I can understand the manipulation and isolation of Corld. It is fun though, isn't it, trying to work it out?" Nobody answered. "Isn't it?" he repeated.

"It is a challenge," said Douglas, "but that doesn't make Corld good."

Tony looked away from Douglas. "What can we change the images into, Ben?" he asked.

"It doesn't matter," Ben replied. "You do not even need to understand the idea or image. They are near dead here because they cannot change. Any change you can create will put life back into the images and we can move on through that."

Ned looked around. "So we can pick anyone we want."

A bubbling voice was beside Ned's ear. "I have the perfect one," Peter offered enticingly, "come with me."

"That will mean we are stuck with you forever," Douglas said, staring sternly at Peter who managed to look quite indignant while quivering gently. "Why should I stay with you?" he demanded.

"Once the idea has life, and I understand what directions it can go, you are on your own."

"No we aren't," argued Ned. "You said yourself, you are directing the idea on behalf of Corld."

Now Peter looked surprised. "Did I say that?"

"Yes," insisted Ned, "and you could be so much more…more purple…if you let the image take other directions."

Peter squatted onto himself, collapsing like a sand castle. "Change," he sneered, "okay, go ahead change something."

"Who is this guy?" asked Tony.

"I think he is an idea police," said Ben. "Works for Corld, ensuring the ideas and images follow the directions Corld wants them to."

"Do you think it is possible to find other directions here, ones Corld doesn't want?" Ned asked Ben.

Ben was looking at the purple mould that still managed to look scornful. "Let's find out. Let's change something."

Douglas pointed to an image. "I have been watching that one. It seems to be pulsating as well as decomposing. How can that happen?"

They walked over to the image. Tony looked back at his engine, still slowly revolving, before following. "Can you hear swearing?" asked Tony when he caught up with them.

"Very explicit swearing," said Ben, "An excellent sign of life so maybe the idea has a spark still."

Ben was correct except that the boy was a girl. She was frantically working her image, shouting at it when it wouldn't do what she wanted and suddenly she threw something and the image broke up even more. The boys stared, all wondering what she could have picked up in Corld to throw.

"Get back together and we will try again," she demanded of the pieces of her image.

Surprisingly, it was Peter who spoke first, a purple haze radiating from him. "What are you doing here?" He sounded as cross as the girl.

She swung around. She was wearing very thick-lensed glasses and still she squinted at Peter, then dismissed him with a nod.

"You again! The revolting Vassel is with you no doubt."

"No, he is not. He is where you should be. How did you get here?" he repeated with even more anger. Peter turned to Ben and the others, all silent and open mouthed in their surprise at this familiarity. "It always seems to be the girls," Peter remarked with a sigh. "Seth first made the suggestion they should be banned and I am beginning to agree. But Corld cannot differentiate. He only sees the ideas and he doesn't have to deal with the girls."

Douglas cleared his throat. "What did you throw at your images?"

The girl swung around again, this time with astonishment on her face. "You can talk?" she asked, "and have a thought process outside your own ideas?"

Ben smiled. "My name is Ben. First, what was it you threw and second, who is Vassel?"

"Celia," she replied, "and I was hoping it was Vassel I threw," she said. Purple quivered at these words. "It could have been. He likes to agitate me by turning up suddenly and he can be quite small." She looked round at her feet. "Maybe it was just a piece of my image," she finished regretfully. She looked up and peered around, finally settling her magnified eyes onto Ben again. "What do you mean, 'who is Vassel'? You must have one like him if you are here?" She looked quizzically at them. "And why aren't you fixated on your images?"

"We are trying to get out of here and would like to use your image." Douglas was being very polite. He thought it would be best with this girl. "We noticed it pulsating and wondered if it had enough life in it to be changed so we can use it to leave here."

With no argument, the girl stepped aside from her image. "You can do anything you want as long as I go with you to wherever it is you are going."

"Ned," said Douglas, "see if you can use your hacker skills to get inside to that pulse. There must be some kernel of an idea that is making it do that."

Ned excused himself as he slid past the girl. She reminded him too much of Hester to be comfortable about taking over her images. Tony sat down beside him. The images held the secret. He had no idea what that was, but it was only through the images he could contact Cassie or meet up with her again. And as for someone called Bella, he would have to find out about that as well.

Ned was examining the image, rotating it and holding it upside down, poking at it now and then, learning how it was constructed and where the weak spots were. Tony watched, studying how Ned probed the image. He thought he could see the core of the idea and how it was expanded, like looking at an old shack that had gradually expanded in many directions with more rooms. But it had the same flexibility his own engine took on while he experimented with a new idea. He pointed out the expansions of idea to Ned. Soon, they both forgot about Douglas, Ben and the girl as they became absorbed in the way the idea was constructed.

Ben folded his arms as he kept an eye on Tony and Ned. He didn't want them to disappear. They had both taken on that look of intense captivation that Corld demands. They would never notice any sign they may be moving to another site. "Does Vassel encourage your ideas?" he asked of the girl.

She had been scrutinizing this little party that had so unex-pectedly appeared. She was somewhat relieved as she had been getting nowhere with her idea and did not know what that meant. The question brought back to her everything she want-ed to ask them. But first, she pointed to Peter. "Yes and he is one of the Vassels. Don't know what they are called but I called mine Vassel."

Peter quivered again, sending out a purple haze that had a vague bad smell. "Why do you have to name us? We are your ideas. Seth was right," he muttered to himself, "having a name is destructive."

The girl continued, ignoring Peter. "I noticed Vassel when I first arrived. Though not being able to see very well, I knew he was there as he exuded a damp warmth. At first I thought I was sitting in something wet. But that could never happen in Corld because there is no water or anything here. Vassel jumped round my images for a while then disappeared. I forgot about him. Except recently, he has given me a few frights because he is suddenly sitting next to me or appearing in my images, distorting them. And here is worse than ever. There are more of these creatures here than I have seen before."

Ben kept glancing at Peter, not wanting to have his attention distracted from Tony and Ned. "That is because the ideas are in trouble here. They are reaching their end. These creatures try to keep them alive as they are the embodiment of the ideas. If the ideas die, they do as well or move elsewhere if they can."

Peter dissolved into a smaller mass of purple at these words. "There are always the small ones," he said quietly.

The girl looked thoughtful. "Do you really think they represent the ideas? Vassel is a very ugly creature and I am sure my idea was quite magnificent." She paused for a while. "Though it was to be used for revenge. Maybe that affected his looks."

"No," said Ben, "all the ideas here are manipulated by Corld towards his own purpose. I don't think any of those purposes have a beautiful ending."

"Revenge on who?" asked Douglas, going back to Celia's ideas.

Celia's glasses glinted at Douglas and he wondered where the light came from. She shrugged. "Bullies at school," she replied turning away. "They think they can intrude on my life any time they want. So I thought I would show them what it is like to have arrogant dumb things always there, affecting your life." She turned back to Ben and Douglas. "I give them something that would always be there, in the time they thought was private, when they are at their computers."

Ben studied the image Tony and Ned were still busy dissecting and putting together. He nodded. "An interesting idea. You are not just hacking but adding another dimension. It travels beside the channels in a computer."

"Yes," said Celia, "and I would send disturbances along these dimensions that come into effect when anything is activated on their computers."

Ben waved to Peter who was also watching the image. "Much like these fellows react to the progress of their particular person and idea."

Celia took off her glasses and wiped them. "I never thought of that. But yes. No wonder I could experiment on Vassel."

"You could experiment on one of these creatures?" asked Douglas with surprise bordering on disbelief.

"No doubt that confused him," remarked Ben. "After all, they should be the embodiments of the idea as it progresses. You were using Vassel to create the idea."

Tony shouted, joining in the conversation but not taking his eyes away from the image. "That is the problem here. Your image has pathways that are not part of the whole idea. There are dead ends in your image because you didn't experiment with the image, but with Vassel. There is no continuation of the idea. That is definitely not the way Corld works. The ideas keep going towards a particular comprehension, even the wrong ideas." He turned to Celia. "Ned is trying to make the ideas in these dead ends go backwards to the original thoughts, then send them in another direction. We don't know where that will land us but it will be exciting finding out." Tony turned back to help Ned.

Douglas sighed deeply, looking at Ben. "I am trusting you knew what you were doing when you gave these two," he pointed emphatically at Tony and Ned, "the task of reactivating the image. They tend to forget our need to get out of here in their enthrallment with their own cleverness, exactly how Corld wants them to behave."

"Don't worry, Douglas," said Ben. "Corld encourages enthusiasms. That doesn't mean the enthusiasm has to turn out bad. And Ned wasn't really captured by Corld. He never had images so hasn't come under the influence of Corld's expectations."

Suddenly, the image shrank to the size of a brussel sprout. Douglas sprang forward. "Don't lose it!" he shouted. At the same time Celia gasped. "That is what it looked like when I started," she whispered.

"No, not quite," said Ned, a spot of calm in the tense anticipation of losing the image altogether. "You had created other pathways through which your invasions moved about when the bullies logged on. Those paths have just contracted but its nub of a beginning is still here. We will travel along that. So," he said turning to face them, "where do you want to go?"

Everyone looked at Tony. He looked surprised, but soon realized Cassie was the link they were searching for. He had to decide which direction would lead to her. Celia's image had been a strange journey. She had created many ideas for causing confusion and unwanted meanings and the image was a conglomeration of these ideas. She didn't try to create one big fear, like bullies generally do. Always threatening with force, their taunts always the same as well since their intelligence was usually limited. All the ideas Celia used would confuse anyone. It is like his plans for fireworks. Trying to make the sounds and effects so varied, people would not know where to look. He was sure the bullies would get angry with the distortion of their messages, the inability to access favourite sites, weird commands appearing on their screens. Especially as they would have no idea why these things were happening and they would be unable to fix it. And there was the sound of an explosion that would occur as soon as they turned on their screens. Tony grinned. It was a good sound as well, like the sudden escape of compressed air. That seemed to activate the formation of the pathways the invasions would take. Cassie would be impressed with that though she wouldn't like the explosion. Something else to scare the animals.

He turned to look back at his engine. He could just see it through odd shaped creatures that had surrounded it. They were probing it, turning it this way and that while they studied it.

"You haven't lost it," he heard Ben say. "Your engine is being looked at and that is what should happen. But it is still there in your mind and you will keep adjusting it to keep it viable amongst all the other influences that exist with it. That is the power of ideas, they can change."

Tony shook his head slowly, looking at Ben. "It did amazing things. I didn't know it could." He turned back to the kernel of an image in front of him. "But not now. Now is the time for Celia's idea." He looked at Ned. "Could we just start from the beginning here? Go where the explosion may take us?"

Ned was slowly debriding the final layers covering the seed of the image. It was difficult work as the image kept falling into itself, hiding the area Ned wanted to expose.

Celia was watching closely. "Do you think you can activate it enough? That core source was the first part of the image to weaken and then everything else collapsed quite fast."

"It should be okay if we can use the remaining force of the surrounding ideas to help it."

"I hope you can fix it, Ned," said Douglas. "If we are going to be exploded, I want it to work."

Ned smiled. "The explosion will be great, Douglas, but I don't know where we will end up."

Ben moved closer to the image, encouraging a reluctant Douglas to stay with him. "It will be change anyway," he observed.

"Hey, are we moving?" Douglas was shouting in surprise and then with concern in his voice, "is everyone here?" A symphony of 'heres' erupted and he thought he caught everyone's voices.

"Something is pulling me," Ned remarked. "Are you all still here?" It was disconcerting. He was looking and looking and couldn't see anyone else. They should all be here in front of him, but there was nothing. He didn't feel as if he was moving, just being pulled away.

"I am here," said Tony, "but you are right. Something is tugging, trying to veer us in a certain direction."

Ned could hear everyone and the voices were having a bit of an argument.

"What would be trying to direct us?"

"Do you think Corld has got hold of us?" Silence followed

this idea.

"Maybe we could move in the opposite direction?"

"I can't remember being aware of moving between sites before."

"I wish the pulling would stop. Especially as we can't see where it is heading."

"At least there are no cliffs in Corld."

Ben's voice sounded strong. "Don't fight the pulling. We do not know what happens if there is resistance. Maybe it separates us."

It was Tony complaining next. "Get off me, Douglas."

"Oh, sorry," said Douglas moving away. "I didn't know. How strange, we can't feel the weight of each other in Corld." He was looking at everyone else lying haphazardly as if they all had tumbled out of a tree. "Well, we can see each other again which means we must have arrived somewhere."

The turmoil of the arrival produced many exclamations but one sounded familiar, surely it couldn't be.

Tony looked up but standing in front of him was a numeral, the number 3, and it seemed to be examining him.

Bella

The feeling of no control swamped Bella even though she knew she was not moving. Just being aware could only mean they had arrived somewhere. Her eyes were shut still. Taking deep breaths, she opened them. Chaos reigned and she remained quiet for a bit longer to gather a calmness. Soon, she realized her vision was fine and she could clearly see the anarchy around her. Swirls of vapour and colour fled from their presence, returning with added swiftness. Bella felt they would hurt if she passed through them. She took another breath. It is only fog with colour she decided. But then something did slam into her. It was like the rapid closing of a door that produces a thick wind and pops the ears. She noticed Grease elongated and trying to pull back from what looked like a black hole. She remembered all the belongings her children had inexplicably lost and she moved towards Grease, not knowing how to help but not wanting him to fall into the hole of all lost things. Thankfully, he managed to compress into a lump once again and stayed close to the shelter of her physical presence. Dots flew everywhere and she hoped it was *therefore* and the erratic flying was intentional as she couldn't see how they were going to collect him together again.

"It is very turbulent here," remarked 3 who himself was a calm and still point in the tumult of this site.

Grease slithered round Bella, enclosing her in a spiral cage. "There is much change here," he said. "Nothing is staying the same." He collapsed into a tar coloured lump at Bella's feet. "It is difficult to maintain my stability," he continued as he dissolved into a pool of slime.

Bella couldn't imagine what horrible thing could happen to Grease but she hoped it wouldn't. She curled her toes, testing her own physical well being. They felt cramped. She focused on 3 who seemed to be as solid as a rock. Except for a couple of dots scrambling to stay perched on 3's upper appendage.

"There are boys over there," he said. Bella followed him as a dot whizzed around. Now she noticed her vision cast a beam in the direction she looked. With the light and confusion here, it wasn't noticeable all the time. But handy, Bella thought, at least she would be able to see if darkness ever became part of the confusion. There was a slight tugging at her hair which finally stopped with a small sigh. The dot had caught in her hair but settled, seeming to consider this a safe place from which to view their surroundings. The other two dots leaped from 3 and soon, Bella felt more struggles in her hair and then quiet.

"Not only is it rough," complained *therefore,* "but nothing makes sense."

Bella could feel a small spot of heat in her hair. She hoped *therefore* would not burn up with indignation. "Is this Corld?" she asked. "You would think it would be impossible for any idea to grow here."

She noticed the boys were oblivious to the chaos that surrounded them, but then wondered if they ever looked around to notice. They did look odd, sitting so still, a contradiction to the movement all around them.

"You would think creating chaos would require similar exertions from the boys," she said aloud.

Grease, who was probing parts of himself into the melee, said he didn't think the boys were intentionally causing the eruptions and disturbances. "There is no content here. These are not their ideas," he suggested as he pulled back from an abyss that had opened up near Bella.

Bella looked around but could not see a complete image, a whole concept, unless you considered chaos to be an entity.

"Where are their ideas?" she asked.

"If not here," said 3, "they must be elsewhere."

"But Corld controls all that," exclaimed Bella. "The boys have to be with their ideas don't they?"

Bella's hair pulled painfully as *therefore* freed all three dots from their entanglement. "This chaos is change," one dot bold with fury, declared. "But there is no sequence to it, so the ideas must be elsewhere. We need to find them." The last words became fainter as all three dots buzzed off in the direction of the nearest boy.

As they moved to follow *therefore,* the boy slowly turned to stare. He seemed unaware of *therefore* moving as a blur in his vicinity but the lights from his eyes folded around Bella and her companions and they were captured in his beam. Again Bella wondered at this confidence amongst the chaos of change. But understandable if he is the instigator. The light moved away from them and once again concentrated on an area in front of the boy.

Therefore came back to hover beside Bella, and she was surprised enough to take her attention away from the boy. She couldn't remember when she had last seen *therefore* in his proper configuration. Except that he was upside down, he was as he should be, an isosceles triangle.

"What did you see?" asked 3.

"A future. His idea is in the future." Abruptly, *therefore* broke up and seemed to be everywhere. Eventually all the dots formed a line that vibrated accompanied by a slight whine. "But there are no events leading up to the future he has created." All three dots dropped suddenly at Bella's feet. "There is no sequence," he ended miserably.

3 extended his lower glyph, scooping *therefore* into his curve.

Grease elongated into a shiny spring. "Is it possible to see a link, even if there is one, when there is so much happening at once?"

"It is in the nature of *therefore* to see a link," answered 3.

"But maybe he does have to be brought into the equation first. If nobody asks, there does not have to be a cause and effect."

"But if it happens, there must be a link," suggested Grease.

"Recognising a link, which is what *therefore* does, is not the same as assuming there is a link because somebody has told you there is one," said Bella. "That seems to be what Corld is good at, convincing the boys of a natural progression of ideas according to his priorities and in the absence of logic and morals."

Bella had moved next to the boy and was unashamedly peering over his shoulder into his images.

"What do you want?" the boy asked peevishly.

"To know what you are doing," answered Bella calmly.

The boy's eyelight caught her so that she blinked. His eyelight on her own was painful for her. She shut her eyes.

"Why are you here?" he asked.

Bella didn't say anything, not wanting to speak under his glare. Even the pleasure of looking into someone's eyes as you talked with them was distorted here.

But the boy didn't really want to know Bella's answer. He knew it was not going to be worth the effort of listening to it. He wanted to explain how clever he had just been. He has succeeded and he had turned instinctively to show off to someone before he remembered he was in Corld where nobody cared about what anyone else was doing. But his eyelight had picked out this odd assortment of beings: a number, a mound of substance and a woman old enough to be his mother. Why couldn't she have been younger and pretty so she would admire him while he explained what he had done? Or better yet, another boy who would appreciate what he had done and they could become friends through their successes with their ideas. He sighed. But there was only this old woman. Still, she would be able to see how clever he is. He will enjoy confusing her with his intelligence.

"I have been awarded the Abel Award for mathematics," he said with a grin, still trying to believe it himself.

"Oh," replied Bella, inadequately. She had not thought of

Corld as having the personality to hand out awards. To keep them just out of reach, yes. She gathered herself to become the encouraging adult she should be.

"Congratulations. When will it be presented?"

The boy glared at her, his eyelight defiantly moving over her face. "Don't be stupid," he said. "It is the *Abel Award*, surely you know. It is presented to those under forty years of age who have shown genius in mathematical calculations. I have done this but not for another ten years." His eyelight returned again to the swirling mass of nothing in front of him.

Therefore had recovered and was now buzzing in her hair again, teasing it into tangles.

"It is the future remember," *therefore* whispered close to her ear, "he is changing the future to suit his purposes."

"Can that work?" asked Bella. "Can Corld really influence what happens outside, I mean in the real world?"

"It may depend on whether the boys can leave Corld," suggested 3. "We haven't seen an indication of that yet." He was silent for a while. "But we do think you and your children can leave here, so why not the boys when Corld requires it of them."

Bella raised her hand to stop her hair from moving, then remembered *therefore* and relaxed again.

The dots hissed excitedly into both her ears, performing in perfect stereo. "This site must be a connection to your world. The boys that are here have worked their ideas well enough for the next step, a return to your world."

Bella was shaking her head trying to comprehend what it was Corld was capable of. She was just getting used to Corld influencing information so his ideas dominate. But now it seems he can also physically act on that by returning boys to the world and there they can speak of and act out his ideas. And more importantly, they are children and youngsters, those who are imaginative and have the energy for rebellion.

"Your monsters should not be here," the boy was speaking with authority but also with a whine. He looked down at 3. "And they are stupid shapes for monsters anyway."

What was he talking about, but one thing at a time she thought.

"Where will you be presented with your award?"

"Overseas somewhere," he replied carelessly.

"Will you be there to accept it?"

"Of course I will," he replied contemptuously. After a brief silence, he added in a quieter tone, "after I have discovered how to leave here."

"Do you know you can leave here?" Bella asked.

"My idea has left here. If that happens, you know you have succeeded and Corld expects you to leave to follow the idea through." He turned to face Bella, not bothering to keep his eyelight away from her own. "Everyone knows that. That is why they are here." His beam seemed to become interrogative again.

"Please, can you stop looking directly into my eyes. My name is Bella, by the way. And what would yours be?"

"Pasquel," he replied, obligingly keeping his eyelight turned away.

Bella still felt uncomfortable. Nothing seemed right in Corld. How can a conversation be conducted without misunderstandings if there is no eye contact or interacting gestures. 3 and Grease were perched on what Bella supposed to be a solid table in front of Pasquel, though it did not have a discernable shape or the look of solidity. Grease was extending his substance into the whirlpools and 3 was watching the results. *Therefore* pulled occasionally in her hair. Bella sat on the floor, Pasquel was on a chair, but if there was to be no eye contact, it didn't matter where she sat as long as she was in talking distance. 3 and Grease would let her know if they discovered anything.

"Ten years is a long time. How do you know everything will happen that leads to you receiving the prize?" asked Bella.

"I am worried about that too," said Pasquel thoughtfully. "I will be twenty-seven years old then. It is too old, too far into the future. The trouble is the award is only presented every four years. I have missed the previous one and if I accepted the next one I would have only two years to consolidate my mathematical theory."

Bella realized he was thinking like any teenager. It wasn't the idea of not succeeding that daunted him but the concept of time. How slowly it goes for the youngsters and how old anyone over twenty-five seems to them.

"So, unfortunately it has to be six years. That is a more realistic time frame and I will be young enough to enjoy it, just." He turned towards her and smiled in her general direction.

Bella couldn't help smiling with him. Too old at twenty-seven to enjoy life. She looked up at him, again intent on the maelstrom that was in front of him. She wondered what enjoyment Pasquel had out of life before he arrived in Corld. He would have had to spend many hours in front of the computer to crystallize his ideas and for Corld to have noticed him. She thought she knew how teenagers behaved. They were frustrating and sometimes unattractive in their self-centered view of the world, but then endeared themselves all over again as, by considerate actions, they showed they remembered there were other people and beings in the world. But the boys she had met here, they didn't care about the others surrounding them, didn't even know they existed. Maybe Corld was encouraging this behaviour. It would help in influencing ideas along a predetermined path. Bella watched 3 communicating with Grease as they examined a small contusion in the space in front of them. Strange that she should feel more confidence in the presence of these two strange creatures, one shaped like a three, than she did in the motives of a child of her own shape.

"How will you know you will still be interested in your maths theory in ten years time?" asked Bella. "You are still young and there is so much in the world to discover."

She knew straight away this was the wrong thing to say. It sounded too much like cautionary advice, hindering the energetic young for fear of them hurting themselves, or worse, not knowing their own minds.

"Mine is a brilliant idea. One that needs to run its course for the benefit of human knowledge." Pasquel's eyelight quivered over her as his angry tones rang out.

Bella sighed. How grand the words sounded and how mean-ingless they were without specifics.

"How do you plan to go about achieving successes to win the medal when you go back?"

Bella listened as Pasquel told of his entry into the elite uni-versity, the challenges of like minds and overcoming their doubts, his theory finally acclaimed for its brilliance.

"But you could have done all that without the help of Corld."

"No," Pasquel commanded. "Corld has encouraged me. Only in this world could I have expanded my idea, seen all the variations and known what to chose."

Bella couldn't argue about the encouragement. It was what everyone needs. "Will Corld be supporting you in the outside?"

"Corld will be there in the award. That is the support," Pasquel insisted.

"Ideas cannot develop in a vacuum. Even spending a lot of time at the computer as you must have done already, your the-ory will still be influenced by the annoying distractions of the outside and also the moments of beauty you discover. Like…the brightness of a beautiful day, the joy of swimming in the surf, people laughing together…." Bella ended lamely, feeling like a pious fool. "What I am asking is how can you develop your the-ory when it will be open to many more influences and contra-dictory ideas than it is here in Corld?"

Pasquel's eyelight was concentrating on the turbulent mass in front of him. "The prize is the encouragement," he repeated. "There will be no difference."

Bella thought again. Reclusive people can be geniuses, so why should it be different on the outside for Pasquel? Because Corld is involved. This world holds menace and because it deals with ideas, the menace is in the manipulation of ideas it sends outside. But what does Corld want to do outside? Is Pasquel important to Corld or the fact of the award? The award will give initial authority to any further ideas Pasquel (or Corld?) may introduce. Bella was beginning to trip over all her thoughts.

Maybe Corld was innocent and it was encouragement only. *Therefore* was teasing her hair again with his agitation.

"Pasquel's future is real," he buzzed into her ear. "There is no sequence but that doesn't mean it will not happen." Bella could not detect dejection in *therefore's* tone, he sounded quite excited. "If something happens, people will justify the sequences themselves." Silence fell on her ears before *therefore* resumed. "I could be anywhere causing anything to be obvious even if it isn't logical."

3 spoke from his place in front of Pasquel. "You would have to deal with the equation itself. I can see into the future and the past here, Bella, through the numbers and symbols in the equations. It is a pathway of calculations leading into future ideas. But some numbers are not happy. They do not want to be standing where they are. It is wrong for them." 3 turned to Bella. "I can see a way to control a journey through Corld. The numbers will help me."

"Are the numbers part of the ideas?" Bella asked.

"Yes." 3 tried to explain. "The people here only have one idea each but the ideas are joined by Corld's manipulation. Grease and I could track back to the idea of Tony and Cassie."

Therefore moved her hair again. "There will be sequences to be found there. Maybe Corld is trying to grow strong enough to hold sequences into the long future, not just in the next few months."

Pasquel had been staring at 3 and now he turned suddenly to Bella, blinding her with his eyelight. "How did you get here?" he demanded.

"I accidentally fell through to Corld," she replied, not seeing how the truth could be dangerous.

The eyelight grew broader on Bella's face. He must be opening his eyes wide, she thought.

"You mean you have no ideas? You are in Corld with no images? How did you know what to do and where you were?" he tried to continue to sound commanding but there was disbelief in his voice. He removed his eyelight from Bella's face and turned it towards 3 and Grease. "I thought these were odd shapes for monsters. What are these things?" The aggression was back.

"We are searching for my children," Bella replied.

Pasquel snorted with contempt. "The people in Corld do not want to be found. Only in Corld can they express themselves."

Bella could see trying to convince Pasquel of any malignant intent on the part of Corld would be useless. So she referred back to yet another comment about monsters.

"What do you mean by monsters. What are they?"

She had surprised Pasquel again. "Everyone here has a monster. It keeps the ideas growing."

Bella remembered the Saedi. Maybe Pasquel thinks 3 and Grease are my Saedis.

"I am only here to find my children and leave."

"You know how to leave here? You will take me as well. When do we go?"

"His future world may not be yours." *Therefore* had broadened his own concept of consequences now.

Bella stood up. "Leaving here is not going to happen until I say so. So concentrate Pasquel, on your maths or on finding your own way out." She bent down towards 3 and Grease. "Do you think you could find the children's path?" she asked, trying not to sound too hopefully demanding.

"There are many empty spaces in Pasquel's images," said Grease. "The connections could be tenuous."

"His ideas have made large jumps," said 3, swivelling towards other images. "Maybe there are ideas that are more detailed in their progression."

"If you want an image that is made from many others," Pasquel suggested, "over there," he pointed dismissively, "you can spy on other images. The boy who created it then steals what he wants. He is not there now but that doesn't mean he is not at his images. Sometimes he seems to be in them."

"Maybe his images will give us more information and choice," said 3 enthusiastically as he hopped down from

Pasquel's image and disappeared into the gloom. Grease twirled his way after 3 and Bella could only spot them now and then as the atmospheric confusion of this site gave them a strange glow. "Be careful of Corld," she shouted in the direction she had last glimpsed them. From somewhere very different came a reply, "Oh, we will." Then everything seemed very quiet.

"There is no need to be careful," said Pasquel, breaking the silence, "Corld will look after them. Unless of course, they want to damage his ideas in any way," he finished with a suspicious flick of his eyelight over Bella.

"No," sighed Bella, sitting down beside Pasquel again, "they won't do that." She cast her eyelight in the direction of the other boy's images. "But what is that boy doing at this site? I would think if Corld is as helpful as you keep insisting, he would not tolerate messing with other boys' ideas."

Pasquel shifted in his chair. This conversation was not going to plan. Things were happening that he didn't understand and that should not be in Corld. This world is his support and opportunity. Nobody should be in here that questions his ideas, or even worse, the workings of Corld.

"I am sure Corld knows what he is doing and gets something in return," he stuttered. Bella watched as he took a deep breath which also seemed to fill him with his usual confidence. "Lots of ideas are encouraged, one being how to make them grow faster and to be strong with influence. That boy has been experimenting with that. I asked him if there was a way around the time delay in receiving my award."

Her hair blew into her face, except that it was *therefore*. Bella had forgotten about him and now he was humming in her ears again. "Corld must be impatient for results. After all it takes a long time to change the way people think. First, they have to get used to thinking about cause and effect and alternatives and then the idea they can change."

"But how do you speed up that process? Corld could not put out ideas that were blatantly manipulative and violent. He would have to prove some wisdom for his ideas to be accepted."

"Not necessarily." *Therefore* was buzzing around her hair again. "The first action is to be able to manipulate these boys because of their lonely need for encouragement and their search for self esteem. And he is successful in doing so because he is keeping it simple. Much simpler and faster than the same process would be outside because he can shield the boys from criticism and confusion and let them focus on one idea. There are no extraneous influences here. The boys are encouraged and develop a sense of self through their ideas and there is no flexibility in these ideas. It just follows the plan Corld wants of it. It becomes a doctrine, something that is believed without questioning it. Corld then sends them outside and remember, he has already gained support outside from those who access his sites."

And then, Bella thought, the boys would act like small Corlds. There were the insecurities, cowardice, fears and brilliance that are all part of the human mind and they could be manipulated and directed. Also they gain confidence through the support of others, especially as their numbers grow. To encourage and manipulate the boys to this extent, Corld could not rely on the power of suggestion from his own mind. A physical presence would be necessary.

"Pasquel, tell me about the monsters you have found here." Bella waited, the silence lengthening and she wondered if she had only thought the question.

Pasquel moved his eyelight over Bella's face and hair. "There is a continual noise emanating from you. Do you have another monster here?" The eyelight moved to and fro as Pasquel shook his head. "They are strange monsters. I have never known them to be friendly and helpful."

"They are not part of Corld," explained Bella. She paused as she figured out how to describe them. "They form the text of the computers, sometimes here in Corld, other times in the computers...uh...the other computers of the outside."

"How can it be they are here with you, offering ideas?" asked Pasquel. "If they are the text, they make up our ideas. They are inert tools we use to create things. They cannot think for themselves. If they could, how would we know what the ideas really mean?"

"But they are not inert because they mean something," protested Bella, against all her own logic. "A three is a three and you cannot use him in an idea that requires a four. If you do so the three becomes a disruptive part of the idea, destabilizing everything. The three grows, demanding attention, but only because it is wrong."

Pasquel was quiet, before answering in a whisper. "They do sound like some sort of monsters."

Bella shrugged. It was possible to make them sound as such. "What do yours do?" she asked.

"They are not really monsters. They help us to achieve our ideas. They know the immensity of Corld's resources and they guide us to them. Our ideas grow with their suggestions. If we were honest, we wouldn't get this far without their help."

"Why do you call them monsters, then, if they are your guides and helpers?" asked Bella.

"Because they look horrible. But they are easily ignored. It is only after one has obviously helped with the progression of your idea that you understand how they can help. By that time you know them as monsters and their real name doesn't come as easily."

"What is their real name?" asked Bella, wanting confirmation of her guess.

"Saedi, though they do not like to be called anything. After all, they are only offers of help."

"Sadies," murmured Bella, "They encourage, suggest, do not make demands and are not intrusive. The perfect parents, except the Saedis are influencing the ideas. Maybe the boys do not notice because the Saedis are not in their face over having to bath, eat healthy meals, or be home by certain times. But they are directing the boys towards violence and destruction, with the accompanying mindlessness that accompanies that and this is the world of Corld.

"When did you encounter your first Sadie?" asked Bella.

"They come to you straight away though not many are aware of them because the images and ideas are so good." Pasquel thought for a bit. "The small kids must be frightened. I wonder if they ever get used to them."

"Small kids?" repeated Bella, "how small?"

Pasquel quickly turned to Bella. "I have never seen them and I am sure the Saedi would never harm them, but I have met a couple of boys who can remember being amongst young children. If they were younger than the boys I was talking to, the kids must have been only five, six, seven...," Bella had Pasquel in the steady glare of her eyelight. "But probably eight or nine years old," Pasquel finished weakly.

Pasquel turned away from her eyelight, his own now shining on what appeared to be a commotion beside him. The place seemed to be filled with people, the scene shimmering because the rapidly moving eyelights made comprehension difficult. A boy stood up, momentarily out of all light and his shape and posture were familiar. He bent to speak to another boy still on the ground.

"Tony!" exclaimed Bella. Relief and delight flowed through her, and there was 3, he must have had something to do with this. She scanned the bundle of shapes for Cassie, sure she would see her if only the purple light would stop following her eyelight.

"What is this you have brought with you?" she asked.

"It looks like a number," answered Tony.

"No, not 3. This creature," said Bella.

All eyelights turned onto Peter who was studying them, his purpleness moulded to form a being that exuded disapproval. They watched as a face bulging with frowns etched itself into the purple.

Cassie

Cassie was surrounded by a lot of small children. She guessed the ages to be between five and ten years. Some still carried the chubbiness of the baby years. But they had the alertness of that age group with the candid curiosity for anything new, which at this moment, was her appearance. They were watching her, not Seth, who was bulging a few eyes at the scene around him. Her eyelight also scanned the site. There was a luminosity here that lit up the place. Eyelights were not tracking round so the children's vision must be as normal. As she picked out the children one by one, she felt a keen nostalgia for the vision these children had. And no wonder they were not staring at Seth, as her eyelights were picking out creatures, different to Seth, but to her imagination, holding the same menace. The more she looked the more she spotted. But the children didn't appear to notice them. Cassie concentrated. Now and then it seemed as if the children asked something of the creature next to them and sometimes reached out and touched them, absentmindedly, but still it was a touch. Cassie shivered and returned her gaze to Seth.

"Are the creatures like you a part of this site?" she asked.

"Yes and you should not be here," Seth declared. He started muttering and fidgeting, swiveling his eyes all the time. He was still suddenly and Cassie tried to figure out which eye was staring intently and in which direction. She looked away and spotted the emu instrument creature beside a young boy. He wasn't so emu like now as his neck had inflated and was able to fold like a concertina except that it was up and down not sideways. It was doing so now, though Cassie couldn't hear any sounds. Its body was still plump, held up on stilt like legs. The boy was jiggling in time to the neck of the creature. They looked like they were performing a duet. Seth entered her eyelight, scuttling towards them. Not knowing what was going on, she followed.

There was an image hovering in front of the child. It didn't seem to be as alive as those Cassie had watched when the older kids had worked them. The image was hanging loose in the air and it seemed insubstantial. Though it was moving and chang-ing, it was awkward and hesitant as if it didn't know what was going to happen next. Well, thought Cassie, if the image is the idea of this child, no wonder it is not fully formed. He must have thousands of imaginative workings going on in his mind but without the years or experience to formulate the ideas properly. What use could a mind like that have for Corld?

The image did move and the child was watching it and gig-gling helplessly now and then. The creature too was working the image, but it would move about when the child laughed. Gradually, Cassie realized the creature was joining in with the laughter. Seth, meanwhile, was becoming bloated, his eyes weeping which seemed to be an effective lubricant as they were also practically spinning round his torso. An eye would fall out occasionally and left to dangle helplessly, trying to feel its way back into the mulch that was Seth. This must be anger, Cassie decided.

"What is he doing wrong?" asked Cassie, pointing at her creature. Really, he must have a name. He was jovial and appeared good natured and Cassie felt she would like to know someone friendly here. She would think of him as Aaron instead of the creature.

Seth swung round, the movement slapping a couple of eyes against her.

"He is encouraging this child into inappropriate thoughts," he slurred viciously.

Another laugh bubbled from the child. "He seems to be

enjoying them," Cassie remarked.

"They are not what Corld wants," Seth pronounced each word with anger.

"Would he be so happy if he followed Corld?" Cassie asked, but Seth was not listening, busy as he was now with the child and his image. The other creature had stepped politely aside which seemed to infuriate Seth even more and his eyes rotated angrily every time the child looked towards Aaron for confirmation of Seth's instructions.

Cassie leaned forward to better see how the image was being worked and the changes that were occurring. Animals figured. It looked so normal, there was a cow, a giraffe and an elephant as seen by a five year old. Her mum would have enjoyed this. Elephants were the reason she went travelling all those years ago, when she wasn't much older than Tony. She wanted to watch them roam in their own space she had said and did so for another fifteen years and her eyes never lost the misty, faraway look when she told another story from those times. Cassie smiled at the elephant passing before her eyes now. It was also beautiful because it represented adventure and beauty and everything we could be, especially when as a five year old, you believed the beauty would remain alive and with you forever.

Seth nudged her aside and now the elephant was disappearing in a mockery of something wild. It was trapped in a small circle and it didn't walk anymore but just swayed back and forth.

"What are you doing?" Cassie demanded of Seth. "Why is the elephant drawing back?" She stared as a bigger image followed the elephant. She leaned closer, notwithstanding the unpleasant wetness at the touch of Seth.

The child was coordinating his movements with Seth. Aaron had fallen silent. The other image was holding a stick and the elephant, or its caricature, was reacting to it. Cassie looked further. The giraffe seemed to have gone, the cow was standing still, its head hanging down. She wanted to look into its big eyes to know what was going on. But then again, maybe she didn't, it looked like it was suffering.

"What is happening here?" she shouted at Seth. Aaron looked across at her and she was surprised to see sadness in his eyes.

"Leave the child alone!" Seth shouted back at her in a voice brought from the depths of his substance. Cassie stepped back from this vocal onslaught that moved around her head in a tepid stench. But there was more. "He is discovering the position of animals in his ideas."

Cassie forced herself to gaze on the elephant. "Position? What do you mean? His position should be where he belongs, in the wild, free from torment." She wondered at that word, but the image did look like torment.

"No," returned Seth, "that is not important. It is how the child can control and use the animal."

"Not important?" She was still shouting but now was too upset to think of anything else to say. Cassie looked towards the child. He hadn't paid any attention to the commotion around him and under Seth's encouragement, the animals were subdued even further and the child's concentration reminded her of the staring boys she had met at the other sites. The laughing had stopped and suddenly the child sat back, no longer working the images.

"This is not a 'lephant," he said. "It is not waving his trunk and flapping his ears."

Cassie held her breath. The child had noticed the elephant was not behaving as it should and Seth was failing to convince the child otherwise.

But Seth was sitting beside the child now, adding something more to the image. A kindly woman appeared. She was a three dimensional picture but slightly blurry as if she were standing in vapours. She was helping the elephant to move. Watching Seth grinning as this happened, Cassie wondered if this insubstantial person was only leading the elephant to further suffering. It worked with the child though. He also gently touched the elephant to make it move forward.

Cassie leaned towards them, pushing Seth off the bench. He

landed with a dull splash and the child stared at Cassie. The woman had moved away from the images and when the child noticed this, he hurriedly worked to get her back. His little fingers clumsy with his haste and inexperience, gradually the woman disappeared. He turned to face Cassie, his eyes, shiny with tears, sparkled in the glow of the site. She didn't know what to do, though she was sure the woman would inflict more hurt on the elephant but the child didn't understand it that way. To him, she must have been helping. Her eyelight searched for Seth and there he was, still on the floor, leering up at her. She wanted to shout at him but knew somehow the child would see this as more aggression on her part. Seth quietly squirmed his way between herself and the child and regained his control over the images.

"There was suffering in those images," Cassie hissed at Seth.

Seth guided the images so they would again be understandable to the child. "No," answered Seth in a new agreeable tone. "Corld is teaching him how to have ideas and how to develop them."

"But why does the child need teaching? Just let him explore all the ideas."

"Corld is encouraging the child. That is not wrong."

"Manipulating him you mean," said Cassie.

"As you were when you tried to help," replied Seth evenly.

The elephant was now thrashing about as the child encouraged him on. It is only an idea, thought Cassie, not a real elephant. There is not real hurt there. The child was silent with intent. But what is he learning, wondered Cassie. To her it looked like cruelty.

She balled her fists in helpless frustration and looked around. Aaron was moving away towards another child.

Why did the child react so differently when Aaron was sitting next to him? "Who created you?" she asked Seth.

"Corld did."

"Why are you different to Aaron?"

"I come from the mind of one particular boy," explained

Seth. Cassie remembered watching something roll away from Tony. Then Seth had been there. "You are the manifestation of Tony's ideas," she exclaimed. "But why have you been following me?"

"Tony has good ideas and he is smart. He didn't need my help. You are similar and you had nothing. I wanted your ideas to come out and grow." Seth scowled at her. "But you do not help. You dismiss all ideas. I should have left you for Corld to fix."

Cassie was thinking. "But there is Aaron." She watched Seth's eyes grow large as they flicked light at her. "Aaron is...me!" She went towards Seth and actually grabbed him. "But I didn't have any ideas. What is Aaron?"

Seth seemed to slump into a rounder lump. Just like Tony when he doesn't want to do something. "Corld will not be happy with Aaron," Seth lamented. "You do not have any ideas Corld would want to use so Aaron doesn't either. He may be disruptive."

"Isn't that good? Because some of these ideas are terrible. Even some of Tony's ideas are not worth following through."

All of Seth became big now, even his contours and wrinkles disappeared. His colours glowed and Cassie wished they were not quite so bilious looking, especially as Seth seemed to spit some out in his rage. "Tony has ideas worth encouraging. You will not be involved."

She looked around. "Who is involved here? Are these the creatures from the children's ideas?"

"They are too young to have ideas useful for Corld. They were enchanted by the computer screen and Corld brought them here to be influenced by the ideas of others. When they are old enough to formulate coherent ideas, they will have their own Saedi to encourage them. The Saedi," Seth pointed to himself, "visit here when they are not needed for the images of the older children."

Cassie watched the children, trying to see some indication of how long they had been here. Seth was right about their enchantment for the images, though there was nothing else here to gain their attention. Maybe that was what it was like in their homes, only the computer for company. Maybe it wasn't puppy fat she had observed but fat gained from hours in front of the computer. There was so much else in the world...well not this world. Were they not shown that? She decided to find out. She tried to pick out a child, scanning the site carefully. She was startled to realize how many creatures like Seth there were here, they were all interacting with the children and the children were accepting their presence and their influences. The children were so much younger than her but they looked like they belonged here. They knew what they were doing, whereas she still had no idea.

She approached another child and only spotted the Seth like creature when she was close to the images. She inspected the Saedi, wondering if she had met the boy whose ideas had made this one. The creature stared back at her with curiosity but that may be because she wasn't supposed to be here, as Seth had mentioned. She turned her attention to the child. She sighed as she sat down. The child's attention was on his images with the same intent she had seen in the other, older boys. She was learning about conversation and how it needed more than one willing person. Still, maybe nobody had talked to this child with interest so he could, in turn, learn how to talk to other people.

His name was Dougal. Cassie looked up at the creature who shrugged his substance instead of the shoulders he did not have.

"That is a good name," she replied, "mine is Cassie."

But all other questions he ignored. She can't get him to talk about any pet he has, any holiday he has been on or even where he lives, if it is in the country or not. She doesn't know if this is because Corld has taught him not to remember or if he doesn't have a pet, has never been on a holiday and has never stepped out the door of his house. Well, he probably wouldn't do the latter without one of his parents. Maybe for all those things to happen you need an adult who loves you to show you the wonder of it all or to help you to care for another being.

Cassie looked to the images. It wasn't animals or crude pictures as drawn by children. There were mathematic symbols and what looked like architectural designs. Gravity seemed to be suspended in some of the designs. A large rectangular block teetered on its pinnacle. Cassie watched the suspense along with the child and the creature. When nothing happened, Cassie started to wonder if it was supposed to be balancing precariously, always teetering but never falling. Suddenly it fell and exploded open, showering small coloured grains that landed on them all. The bulk fell at their feet and from there, it moved away, making a tinkling noise as it did. The child was laughing and the creature was looking exasperated.

"Was that supposed to happen?" asked Cassie.

The child looked at Cassie and shrugged his shoulders. "No, but it is fun."

"Do you want the bigger shapes to stay on top of the smaller ones?" she persisted.

"They not want to, but I can make them." He waved his chubby arm at the equations.

Cassie looked closer and checked the calculations of a few. Some were beyond her (and she looked at the child again) but the ones she could understand were all correct.

"What does this one mean?" She pointed to an equation that nearly looked familiar. She couldn't quite see how the answer came about.

The child's eyes lit up and he leaned forward. "My flying, to somewhere else."

"Using what?" asked Cassie.

The child was looking at her with a frown creasing his face. "Nothing," he said. "I just go." Cassie concentrated on the equation, remembering she was in a computer. Maybe it was for going to another site. But this calculation was standing on its own. There was not a continual progression of ideas for it to gain momentum to shift sites. She put her finger to another calculation. Immediately the creature was beside her and she felt his pressure on her hand.

"Do you want to go to another site?" she asked. The child looked at her with incomprehension.

"Not one, all of them." He went back to his images, now concentrating on the equation Cassie had touched. She wondered if she had ruined it. She reached out for the calculation immediately behind the one the child was now working. She tried to ignore the menacing presence of the creature. Then she forgot everything as she saw the meaning, but it was slightly out. She picked out a three and put it elsewhere, but it kept returning. Now there were chubby fingers correcting her interference.

"This three, though," Cassie explained, "shouldn't be there." The child sat back, unable to push aside Cassie's larger hand. She worked for a bit longer then realized the child was climbing down from the bench. "Don't go," she exclaimed but he had wandered off, the creature following and staring at Cassie as it went. The child had been upset with her, probably considering her an interfering older person who thought she knew best and didn't even listen. She had probably been acting like every adult the child had encountered in his short life, an impatient grown up and he had given her the greatest insult that is possible in the child's world, to just walk away. Cassie sighed. How was she going to move on from here? She wasn't helping anyone and she was running out of ideas. The three was persisting in staying at the wrong end of the equation. She thought she would correct it for the child. It was the least she could do. The calculation wouldn't stay corrected and she started to lose confidence in her own ability to add. She slammed down her hands in frustration, taking her eyes away from the calculations. And now there were flies annoying her. She impatiently tried to bat them away. But flies, she thought, here in Corld. Not possible. Slowly she looked up and Tony was grinning at her.

Everyone

It certainly looked like Tony grinning that stupid grin. But everything was moving around and flickering with lights. It was difficult to concentrate on one thing. Cassie thought maybe she was imagining Tony. She had to be because now he was morphing into one of those creatures and he was all purple, nearly too bright to look at.

"You have finally caught up with us."

It was Tony's voice. Cassie stared just past the edge of the purple and there he was. She stood up, her brother moving forward to help which he turned into a hug. He scanned the area behind Cassie. "Hasn't anyone come with you?" he asked.

"No," Cassie replied, remembering how unexpected her movements always were. Except for when she moved with Michael. That was planned but he didn't continue with it. Oh why didn't he come with her she wondered dejectedly. "Nobody seemed to want to leave their images." She batted at things around her face, "except for these flies," she finished.

Tony grinned even more. "I wouldn't do that to *therefore*. After all, he did help you."

Cassie thought Tony was making even less sense without his images so she looked around instead. There seemed to be a crowd here and her eyes opened wide as she spotted Douglas. She shouted his name as he came towards her, smiling. The purple creature persisted, scowling at her in the same way Seth reacted to her. There were others and Cassie wondered what this site was. Then her mouth dropped open as she saw her mother.

"Mum!" she exclaimed in wonder and relief.

Bella, feeling light with happiness, folded her arms around Cassie

Cassie looked up into her mother's face, still not quite believing she was here, in Corld. And now, even more disbelieving and maybe worrying, Bella was turning towards a number and talking to it as if it was Tony or herself. But everyone was talking at once now so Cassie thought maybe she was wrong about that last impression.

Tony was admonishing her for not paying attention to what he had been doing. "We have been looking for you everywhere," he finished.

Cassie studied his face. "And your machine? Is it here as well?"

Tony blushed a slight pink and then his smile reappeared. "That engine was brilliant. It got us out of some tight spots and was the focus for change so we could move around Corld." His smile lost its shine as he also informed her they had to leave it behind.

"But Celia there," he waved his arm in the direction of a crowd of people, "her ideas do not require a mode of transport, they are the transport."

Cassie could make out another female in a group talking to others she didn't know. And she also seemed to be talking to a number three and Cassie was sure that mound of stuff was listening as well. She looked up at her mother, still there and seeming to have transfixed the purple creature who wasn't moving far from Bella's side. Douglas stood beside Cassie but before she could ask what was happening, Bella's clear voice broke over the chatter.

"I would like to return home." She held everyone in her gaze. "If each of you could say what it is you would like, we can decide how best to go about everyone's plans."

Tony could be heard muttering about his engine, but it was Ned who spoke out first.

"I would also like to go home. Hester must be nearly mad with not knowing what has happened and what Corld is and I may have been part of all that worry at times." He looked to Bella. "I will leave with you to the outside and plan again when we get there."

"Of course, Ned. So where is it you do live?"

Ned watched Bella's surprise as he mentioned his home-town. "Is it far from you?" he asked.

"Yes, in another state, just over 1000 kms, I'd guess." She shook her head. "But that is only relevant if we end up at our place. Everywhere could be a long way from Corld in directions we may not even know yet."

At this, Tony's eyes lit up. "You found other levels around Corld, Mum, so there could be many other sites coming from different angles. Gosh, there could be anything."

Bella sighed. "Could be Tony. But the plan is we keep going till we get home. No stopping." She looked round at the faces, all automatically nodding in agreement, some even intoning 'Yes, Bella.' She smiled at herself, knowing their compliance was probably only politeness. The journey home could also be long, though no doubt interesting.

Cassie could only stare at these people who seemed to know each other and her mother. She spotted Ben, looking as if he belonged in Corld. She asked Douglas who he was. Douglas followed her dim eyelight. "Oh, Ben," he declared. "We met him at the dead site. He thinks Corld is a simple world, just very manipulative." He looked down at the confusion still on Cassie's face. "Ben says everyone here only has one idea and that makes it very easy to direct this one thought in the way Corld wants. With no other influences, the ideas and hence Corld becomes stronger."

Cassie was nodding now. "But why is he here?" she asked.

"He comes to rest his mind. I think his mind makes him go mad." Douglas was shaking his head at the strangeness of Ben. "He is such a good fellow, a real friend."

Bella had been listening to Douglas talking of Ben and remembered Cassie came here by herself. Her experiences would have been different to how Tony and Douglas travelled through Corld and she may have seen things the boys had not. She spoke up again. "We have all arrived at this particular place in Corld through different routes." Her scan of the faces included Pasquel, who was staring intently at everyone. "So if anyone thinks what is said may be wrong or can be done differently, please speak up."

It was Peter, his purple blazing, that accepted Bella's invitation. "Everything that happens in Corld is noticed," he said with a hint of threat. "What you are doing now is not right."

Bella turned towards Peter, his pulsating purpleness throwing the same blemish onto Bella.

"We are deciding what we can do now, thinking over ideas. Isn't that what Corld is about? Maybe he will learn something."

Peter looked as if he was about to burst but he remained close to Bella and concentrated on the gathering.

"How are we to get home?" asked Cassie.

Bella introduced 3, *therefore* and Grease as they came to stand beside her. *Therefore* collected his three dots and for once working together, tried to push Peter aside. It didn't seem as if Peter noticed and the dots finally stopped and were now dripping a purple colour.

"They are from your mathematical equations, your homework," Bella continued. "When I followed you, it was only to that site I could go. The symbols there were gaining an awareness of their surroundings because Corld is interfering with their meanings. 3, Grease and *therefore* volunteered to help find you and Tony. The other symbols have been keeping the site open as a link back to the bedroom."

"So there is a way out?" asked Cassie.

"Well, we hope so darling," Bella replied.

"But what about Michael and...," Cassie hesitated, stumbling over the names of all the others that must be trapped here and the children. Oh, they couldn't *not* take them. "Can we take others out?"

Ben puts his hands in his pockets, preparing for speech. "I will stay because this place needs more investigation to see how powerful it is and what can be done about all the children here as Cassie quite rightly mentions. I can use Celia's ideas as one way of travel. Hopefully our Corld companions," he bowed slightly to 3, *therefore* and Grease, "can help," he finished.

"I don't understand. How can the symbols move around Corld when they are not ideas?" asked Cassie.

Therefore buzzed around her, one dot falling at her feet. Her attention was then taken by the number 3 and the mound of substance as they approached her.

"Symbols like us are used to formulate the ideas so we can blend into the images to travel and sometimes we can alter ideas," 3 explained.

Cassie stared at 3 while she remembered. "You were part of the equation I was trying to repair and it just wouldn't work. You opened the channel for me to get here."

"Finally Cassie," exclaimed Tony, "it was simple. You really must pay more attention to what is happening around you."

Douglas grinned at her and told her not to worry about what Tony says. "When we first arrived here, we had to explain to Tony what a *therefore* was."

He continued. "I will stay as well and help Ben find out more about Corld."

Ben nodded at Douglas. "Your presence will be valuable," he said. Douglas swelled at these words.

Celia coughed. "I really must go home," she said. "My parents not only worry, but they wouldn't know what to do." Bella stood beside Celia, placing her hand on her shoulder

Cassie spoke up. "This is all very well, Douglas and Ben staying, but how will we know they are alright. We cannot keep watching our computers just in case they are in trouble."

"Agreed," said Bella. "We should know how your investigations are going. Maybe we can share the lookout for any messages from you."

"We can work at the computers in shifts," suggested Ned, "Tony and Cassie, Celia and Hester and myself."

"Good," said Tony, "that means we have to stay in contact.

If we get home that is." He smiled briefly at his Mum but Bella refused to take the bait.

The excited chatter started again as they swapped numbers and addresses and made plans for when they could meet again and fired up each others' imaginations with what could be in Corld and what they would do to fight it.

Pasquel tried to listen to everyone at once because he couldn't believe what they were saying.

"There is nothing here except ideas!" he shouted. Quiet descended as everyone turned to him. "You are wasting your time and efforts looking for some ultimate force here. Corld is just a highly advanced world that can express our ideas through amazing technology. It does not have an agenda for these ideas. You are seeing danger where there is none."

Bella faced Pasquel, trying to see through the glare of their eyelights some sort of contemplation of Corld and their situations. "Why would this world need creatures like Peter if there is no control?"

"They are only encouraging us. There is nothing sinister about them." His eyelight didn't waver from Bella. "As I have explained to you."

Bella sighed and turned away, only to face Peter and the grim smile he was directing at her.

Cassie remembered Seth's appearances, his comments on her efforts more menacing than encouraging. "Seth certainly wanted me to have ideas but only ones Corld would like." Everyone had turned to her, all looking puzzled, except for Peter, whose eyes were moving across his mass in agitation. Finally they were still, though not looking in the same directions.

"You are Seth's creature?" he demanded of her, trying to put Cassie in his glare while he struggled to get more words out. In this silence a babble erupted.

"Who is Seth?" asked Tony. "Why didn't you bring him?"

"I thought Seth's girl was you," said Douglas.

"More idea police," muttered Ben.

"You have only been here a short time,"

But Peter exploded drops of purple over everyone as he finally blurted out words. "Seth may lose his reason for being because of you." He rose and spread a purple tinge over Cassie. "Corld...," the violence seeped out of him, reducing him to his normal size though his purple still pulsated. "Corld has been watching."

Cassie stepped towards Peter, surprised at her concern for Seth's well being. "But Seth is really Tony's engine. He has that to watch over."

"You mean one of these creatures represents my ideas?" asked Tony, his mind on his engine and his eyes trying to picture its travels through the machinations of Corld.

"Yes," said Cassie, "Seth was really yours, he just came to me now and then to influence any ideas I might have. Having no ideas and no images is not good for Corld."

Peter's concentration had not left Cassie. "But you have one now."

Cassie remembered Aaron. "Why yes, I do."

"What did you think of that Corld would be interested in?" asked Douglas.

"Well, nothing that could be called an idea. He was a doodle I suppose and then suddenly he was there, as a real creature." She turned to her mother as she remembered where he appeared. "It was with the children. They have four and five year olds here, Mum. Can't we take them with us? They should be with their parents."

Bella looked towards Ben and then faced Peter who seemed to lighten into a pink for an instance. "What is this about? Why do you need such young ones here?"

"They have ideas too," retorted Peter, trying to move his eyes away from Bella's stare.

"And if the idea is obsessive enough, Corld is able to lure them and entrap the children," Ben finished for him. "The plans we have decided upon are the best courses of action to take to help everyone." He looked at Bella. "There are weaknesses here. Even Peter talking to us is a weakness because he is opening himself up to more than one idea. Then there is Seth who seems to have entangled himself with two different ways of thinking." He turned to Cassie. "And your doodle creature may be interesting to meet."

"Aaron," muttered Cassie. "Yes, Seth wasn't happy with his interaction with the children."

"The ideas themselves could also prove destabilizing to Corld," said Tony. "If Seth is still around that may mean my engine still exists. But what is it doing to Corld now that it doesn't have the original idea to drive it?"

"Your engine may save us all yet," said Cassie.

Tony smiled, ignoring any sarcasm and giving Cassie a friendly neck lock. "The show it will put on while doing so will be worth everything."

"Don't forget to keep an eye on Pasquel's progress. What he achieves could be an indication of how strong Corld is on the outside," suggested Ben.

Pasquel sat straight suddenly, looking enraged at this further insinuation that he is being controlled. But before he could launch into another rage of denial, Bella spoke up.

"And Ben, the boy who steals the images of others, he may be useful if you meet him."

Celia stood beside Peter. "And watch this one. He might seem only a glare of brilliant purple but I know him. He notices things. Don't trust him."

Purple swept across the space before receding to a halo surrounding Peter. He pointed a blaze of colour at Ben. "You will be deleted at the first sign of an idea gone wrong. You are ignorant to stay."

Ben looked around. "Well, I suppose the only thing left is to find out if you can leave here."

At these words, the children seemed to realize they were all saying goodbye. Bella watched as the self consciousness of fondness strained their final words. 3, *therefore* and Grease were beside her again and she found she also didn't know how to express her feelings.

3 saved the situation for everyone by being practical about how they could leave Corld. Grease, after a gently encircling of Bella's wrist, moved away to be next to Ben and Douglas. *Therefore* and Ned arranged themselves beside 3 at the images, with Tony and Celia watching and ready with advice. Soon there was the excited chatter of ideas, remonstrations and other inspirations. 3 wavered in and out of focus while *therefore* buzzed erratically. Bella wondered what consequence would happen if he didn't keep all three dots together. But he had survived so far and Bella knew she was incapable of comprehending infinite effects. Best leave it to the one whose nature it was. Pasquel had sidled up to her though he was torn between staying near and having a closer look at what Ned was doing.

Ned shouted to Celia. "Isn't that where we went previously? It looks very familiar."

Douglas started forward to check as well but Ben restrained him.

"I hope they don't just go back into Corld," Douglas said, sounding worried.

Ben nodded. "They have gone somewhere, anyway."

Douglas stared. They had all gone. The space in front was empty, except for Peter still glowing and Grease, who was partially encircling him, retreating and then trying again from another direction.

"We may as well start our investigations with Peter," said Ben. "Then we can watch him while he watches us."

On the Outside Again

Cassie heard Queenie's bark. She couldn't see anything yet, but how beautiful a sound it was. A cold nose nudged at her neck. She instinctively put out her arm and she was stroking warm fur. Now her eyes could see and over the golden shape, she spotted her father, smiling stupidly at everything. Queenie's barks became more joyous as she found even more people to welcome. Cassie jumped to her feet, ran to her Dad and found herself enclosed in a bear hug.

"You won't believe what has happened," she shouted excitedly.

Justin smiled down at his daughter. "I have been in a state of disbelief for some time now." He looked over to Bella, also smiling and helping more than two children off the floor. "It was Queenie," he said, "she wouldn't leave this room."

"Justin, let me introduce Celia and Ned," said Bella while still talking quietly to them, assuring herself they were fine. She looked round the room. Only the four children. Where was Pasquel?

She turned to the computer. The screen projected a light and there was some blurring around a clearly defined number three. Bella gently placed her finger on the 3. It blazed briefly before fading away. Three fullstops lay at the bottom of the screen. With sudden popping sounds, the dots disappeared into the computer and the light dimmed.

Bella went to Justin, linking her arm with his. "Let's go down and make sandwiches for everyone." She turned to the group of disheveled children. "Tony and Cassie, you can show

Celia and Ned around, please use the phone for as long as you want, then come downstairs for something to eat. We may be able to talk about a few things before you start to feel sleepy."

"Sleep," said Tony as if remembering what it was, "sounds like a good idea if a waste of time."

The children chuckled at each other.

As they made the mound of sandwiches, Bella and Justin could hear their laughs and shouts, interjected now and then with Queenie's bark. Justin was shaking his head a lot, but he only had to listen to the four different voices coming from upstairs to know the adventures Bella was describing had truly happened.